Deedee and Wendell

Yuli Liv

Translated by Yardenne Greenspan

DEDICATION

"How old would you be if you didn't know how old you was?"

This book is dedicated with love and wonder

to all of us that are growing....and growing old......

To Mom and Moshe with love

CONTENTS

FALL

On November 6th, 2013, a Wednesday, the morning of her eightieth birthday, Deedee Field decided it was time to say goodbye to this world. She disconnected the phone, closed the curtains in the bedroom, lay down on her wide bed, and waited. *Death is not far*, she thought. *Only a fraction of a second separates me from it.*

She took deep breaths, filling her chest with fresh air. When she inhaled she could feel her heart expanding. She blew the air out slowly, and once her stomach was completely empty, she took another slow breath in, filled with awe, enjoying time and again the sound of air as it rushed out through the nose, a sound that always reminded her of the one the waves made when they met the shore.

Once, a long time ago, she read that some people who did spiritual work and meditated for years could eventually choose to leave their body, thus controlling their own deaths.

To stop, to cease to exist. *Could I do that too? Perhaps death is not so terrible,* she pondered, lying on her back, the deep breathing making her head spin. *I didn't exist before I was born, either. What if this is the same, only in reverse?*

These kinds of thoughts filled her head that morning. She always knew this would be the best way for her to die—to say goodbye to this world in the midst of deep sleep, at the end of which those invisible golden threads, those very microscopic webs that returned her soul to her body each morning from its nighttime wanderings, would break. Like a helium balloon racing upwards as soon as it is released from its grasping hand—that is the way she wished to release her satiated, exhausted soul back into the embrace of her creator.

She was no longer convinced what made her want to say goodbye to this world before her time had come. Earlier that morning, the rooms of the house were quieter than usual, and she hurried out for a little stroll, hoping to alleviate her loneliness with the bustle of morning outside. As she got dressed, she noticed she was unsettled by bad thoughts. What would death look like? And what would happen if she fell ill and none of her friends would be by her side in her time of terrible need? How awful, to end her life sick and alone, needing a stranger to help her bathe, she thought. She tried to push these thoughts away, beginning to plan her morning errands as she walked slowly down the painfully familiar streets she'd strolled each morning ad nauseam. Soon she would stop at the large neighborhood grocery store to buy vegetables for a soup, as she did every Tuesday. She would also buy ingredients for a cake, because no matter her mood, a birthday cake was a duty on a day like today. It was her annual custom and she would keep it this year as well: she would bake herself a big, beautiful cake, decorate it with candles, light them carefully, make a silent wish, and cautiously blow them out.

That morning, when she got out of the shower, she looked at herself in the mirror, slowly studying the deep wrinkles that had grooved the corners of her eyes, affording her a rather angry look. She walked closer to the mirror, scanned her drooping breasts and ran her hands over and over down her scrawny body, as if testing its perishing parts. *Time goes by too quickly*, she thought sadly. Why does it always have to come down to old age? Indeed, deep inside she didn't feel old at all, but on the other hand she'd never felt very young, either. If someone asked her age, she would probably tell them she was ageless.

She'd often wondered how it was possible to preserve sanity, walking on the face of the earth with the knowledge that our life was a temporary thing; that it could end at any given moment. That every day we had a little less time than we had the day before. It was as if her daughter, Alma, was born only yesterday. She could still remember so clearly the tiny baby looking at her and Benjie with her wide-open blue eyes, curiously marveling at the walls of the hospital room. The eyes of a sage that seemed to have remembered the secrets of creation. Now Alma was so far away. If she hadn't had her picture on her bedside table, she would probably be unable to remember her daughter's childhood, all those long gone memories. Now Alma too locked herself up inside the struggles of her own life, allowing its weight to leave its mark on her, as adults are wont to do. Sometimes she tried to recreate little Alma's image in her mind, but the harder she tried, the more the figure faded away. It was as if the drawers of memory were not built to contain pictures of people or moments experienced with them, but only how those people made us feel. She remembered that all too often she'd let Alma down, the arguments they had over unimportant things, and the complicated relationship that overshadowed the fundamental, pure love between the two of them.

Not too long ago she still had dreams, goals to achieve. Most of them revolved around the poems she'd been writing her entire life, for as long as she could remember. She hoped to publish them one day, harboring a secret desire for others to read them and experience that pleasurable sting of pain caused by great poetry. She dreamt of being famous, traveling all over the world and reading her work in front of strangers in unfamiliar places. But, sadly, she could never find the courage to send her poetry to any publishers. The fear of rejection, along with the feeling that she could have done a better job, never let her go. Countless poems remained in the drawer, collecting dust, while others were erased moments after they were written.

But it wasn't only writing that filled her dreams. Long ago—who could remember when?—she had plans to take a museum tour of New York with her sister Rosie one spring. But Rosie has not been well for a long time—lost in her imaginary world, ill, and in pain. Deedee had a long list of destinations she dreamed of visiting one day. Ireland was one of them, inspired by a picture she saw in a glossy travel magazine, showing blue waves crashing against cliffs. Other images that caught her eye told her of enormous green meadows and an impressive lore of fairies and leprechauns. And there were photographs from Alaska, which taught her she could take a boat ride among breathtaking icebergs and meet whales and seals emerging from the deep sea.

For years, she kept a travel guidebook on her bedside table, reading every night about all those faraway places she longed for. She kept her desire to see all these far flung, exotic locales to herself. Benjie was completely unaware of it. Why did she keep it from him? She could no longer say. Perhaps because that was their way with each other, an unspoken agreement to never share their deepest secrets. Or perhaps she preferred to keep it to herself because they never took trips together. The most distant destination they'd visited in all their years together was the neighborhood café, two blocks away, and even there Benjie used to bury his head in a newspaper as she read one of her poetry books. In spite of her dreams of travel, they both liked the warm routine of suburban life. But this routine was deceiving, and over the years Deedee forgot about the things that brought her joy. With time, almost without noticing, the two of them had sunk into a gray life that made both of them unhappy.

Throughout her entire life, Deedee Field was too skinny. With her matchstick arms and her narrow silhouette, she looked somewhat childish. As she walked, her arms swung by her side, making her look like a schoolgirl. Her delicate, pale features, her large fair eyes, and the braid at the nape of her neck all made her look dreamy. When people spoke to her, they got the impression that a part of her was elsewhere.

When she arrived home from her stroll, she walked directly to the kitchen and forced herself to bake a birthday cake. With pursed lips, standing at the marble counter with the large amber stains burnt into it, she wrapped a white apron around her body and began to stir the ingredients vigorously in a large bowl, pausing to wipe away the tears that had begun streaming down her cheeks.

By the time she finished it was already late afternoon. Deedee waited for the cake to cool, continuing to fight a losing battle against the persistent tears. She meticulously iced the cake with bright red jello, on top of which she carefully placed red strawberries, cut into small pieces. Everyone deserves cake on their birthday, she told herself. And she knew that, though no one but her would see or taste it, she would make sure to make the cake just the way she had back in the days when Benjie and Alma still sat at this table, wishing her a happy birthday and gobbling up the slices hungrily. They had a ritual: whenever any of them had a birthday, Deedee made this cake with the strawberries on top. They would tie colorful balloons around the dining table and sit together for a long time, chatting and congratulating the birthday boy or girl. The time between one birthday and the next seemed always to be getting shorter, passing all too quickly.

***

She must have been lying in bed for many hours, lost in a dream, because when she woke up on the afternoon of her birthday, she still had the sensation of dancing with an angel wearing a plaid suit with white wings sticking out the back. The melancholic flute music that accompanied their dance was broken by the rumbling doorbell, rousing her at once.

Wearing nothing but a thin nightgown, Deedee jumped out of bed with a start and went to the door. Glancing through the peephole, she looked like a cat terrorized by a large dog accosting it in a narrow alley. She lingered for another moment before opening the door, astonished to see Wendell standing before her, his face pale. In spite of his skinny frame and advanced age, his stature and broad shoulders made him look robust and masculine. Before she could say a word, Wendell leaned in, took her in his arms, and wrapped his body around hers in a warm hug.

"There you are," he said with a smile of relief. Without waiting to be asked to come in, he removed his shoes, placed them outside the door, and walked right in.

Deedee looked at him, baffled and a bit embarrassed. Her heart was pounding. How long had it been since she'd last seen him? She couldn't say. In fact, at that moment she could say nothing at all. Her mind grew foggy, as if having lost its familiar grip on reality. Suddenly, she recalled how revealing her outfit was and retreated quickly to the bedroom while mumbling a jumble of indecipherable explanations. Away from his watchful eyes, she used her shaky hands to apply dark red lipstick. It was the lipstick she kept in her drawer for special occasions.

"I'm sorry for just showing up like this," he said. "I tried to call, but you didn't pick up."

She sat down beside him at the round kitchen table and made an effort to smile. "Yes… I disconnected the phone when I went to bed. I was in rather low spirits."

Wendell examined her, noting her lips, which were painted carelessly. She appeared to him somewhat frumpy, but still enchanting.

Deedee smiled awkwardly. Wendell's black eyes were even darker than she'd remembered. But when he smiled, a ray of light shone through them. He still wore those same wire-rimmed glasses that made him look like a philosopher. It had been many years since they'd last seen each other, and they both fumbled for the right words, wondering if they still contained the same parts they'd known in each other way back when, sixty years ago.

"It's been so long. When did you get back to New Jersey?" she asked quietly, trying to recover from the surprise.

"A few days ago. I came back to that old

house I used to live in, down the carob avenue. I tried calling you all week, but there was no answer."

"Oh... I must have been out when you called. Why are you back?" she dared ask.

"No particular reason, I just felt it was time. You're the only one who's stayed here all these years." She thought he sounded a little bashful.

An uncomfortable silence spread between them as they searched unsuccessfully for the right thing to say. Finally, Deedee looked down at her bare feet and said quietly, "I was hoping I'd never wake up."

"Why?" he asked, surprised.

"I'm old, Wendell. Old and alone. What's the point in going on like this? Isn't it better to burn out than to fade away?"

Wendell got up slowly and went to stand at the window, looking out onto the street. He was embarrassed by her sudden sincerity.

Deedee let out a long sigh. "You'll have to forgive me for this somber welcome."

He glanced at the cake in the middle of the table. "Can I have a piece?" He asked, fixing his eyes on the bright red icing. Then, without waiting for an answer, he began cutting himself a nice, big slice.

Outside it was growing dim, the rays of last sunshine filtered in through the light colored curtains, throwing dark shadows across the walls. Deedee got up to turn on the light, feeling that same sadness crawling inside of her. She couldn't decide if she was happy to see Wendell again after all this time. Perhaps it would have been better if he hadn't returned, showing up unnoticed like this, she thought as she watched him, sitting at the table in his ridiculous green suit, chewing loudly. He was well over eighty years old and still stunningly childish, she concluded as she went back into the bedroom to get an oversized sweater. *Two silly, wrinkled old people like us, lonely like dogs in a crowded Russian theatre, barely passing the time they still have left. Is this why he came? To ease his loneliness with mine?*

"Deedee," Wendell called from the kitchen, bringing her back to reality. From the sound of his voice, she guessed his mouth was full of cake crumbs. "On your next birthday I'm going to make you a cake with eighty-one dandelions on it instead of candles."

"Dandelions?" she marveled, trying to disguise her gloominess with an attempt at curiosity.

"Yes, dandelions, those white flowers you blow on and make a wish."

She returned to the kitchen and sat down beside him, wrapping her white hair into a tight bun. "I've never been a fan of birthdays or holidays," she said. "They always make me feel like a traveler arriving in a strange town on a cold night, far away from home. And now more than ever, when each birthday signifies an enormous, inconceivable age… It's like living in a familiar, beloved home that is falling apart before your eyes day after day, and you can't do anything about it." Tears began streaming down her cheeks as she spoke. She pulled a tissue from the box on the table and blew her nose with a trumpet sound, attempting to wipe away the sadness of the day.

Wendell looked at her tenderly. "I understand," he said. My old work horse grows rusty and old with every passing week, but as long as he still gets up in the morning and shows interest in some hay and a bit of alcohol I leave him be, not dwelling on it, just thanking the lord that I'm still here. Or trying to thank Him, anyway. Of course, some days I forget, just like everybody else." With a smile in his eyes Wendell shoved a third piece of cake into his mouth and chewed it loudly. Deedee watched the last of the light at the window. A few squirrels ran around in the yard, carrying in their mouths the nuts that had fallen from the trees, collecting food for the nearing winter.

"The light is gone from your eyes, that old twinkle I used to know," he suddenly said.

She took a deep breath. "I feel like I've lived enough."

"Aren't there still things you'd like to do?"

"No," she answered confidently.

"Have you made all of your dreams come true?"

"Of course not."

"Then you can't go yet."

They used to be friends years ago. And though some people think that platonic friendships, devoid of passion, are not as powerful as other relationships, this was certainly not the case for them. In spite of their platonic status, or perhaps because of it, they enjoyed true intimacy, the kind that allowed each of them to say what they really thought without fearing the other's response. The kind of closeness that siblings often have, and that all too often is missing from romantic relationships.

Unlike her, he didn't have a good memory for dates, nor did he lend much significance to birthdays. On more than one occasion he'd even forgotten his own birthday. In his heart he was a true wanderer, not especially concerned about the fact that one day he would die, and that it most likely would not be too long. He was eighty-seven years old, and at this point death was merely the next phase of his life. His old age was a unique time for him, and he was sorry to discover that for Deedee it was filled with pain and dwindling.

They continued to sit there, side by side, for a long time, barely speaking. The years apart had formed a wall between them.

"I'm tired," she finally said through a long yawn, and walked to her bedroom. She got into bed carefully: lifting one leg and then the other, using a small stool. Wendell followed her in and covered her with the thick comforter. Deedee let out a small smile and closed her eyes. *Old people deserve to feel like children sometimes too*, she thought. They needed someone to tuck them in and kiss them goodnight, just like her mother used to do. The mattress pulled down the weight of her body, inviting her to loosen her aching legs and tired shoulders, if only for a short while. How much love and tenderness there is in the small act of tucking in a loved one.

Wendell sat in the chair beside the bed, listening to the humming of the autumn wind outside as it blew the golden leaves every which way.

"Look at those trees," Deedee whispered. "They've only recently grown their glorious foliage and already they're returning it to the ground."

Wendell stared at the red leaves falling to the

pavement. "Deedee," he suddenly said gravely. "If you could have, would you have chosen to stay thirty years old for the rest of your life?"

She pondered his question for several minutes. "I don't think so," she finally answered. "It would probably be quite boring." She continued to watch the leaves until her eyes closed, carrying her into a deep sleep, still wearing her shabby jeans.

How odd to think that dead leaves can be so beautiful, he thought, mesmerized by their circular movement through the air. He got up and went over to the old wooden desk on the opposite end of the bedroom, right beneath the window. This was where she'd been writing her poetry for the past thirty years. Countless small, yellow, wrinkled pages were strewn about. Personal poems, revealing aspects of her personality she'd shared with no one. Wendell tore out a small pink page from a notebook and wrote:

You've been cooped up in your blue-gray house for too long, living life through the windowpanes.

Have you closed yourself off from the world to keep people out? Or perhaps, to see who would still insist on coming in?

I've been thinking, in light of our conversation today… maybe most people don't really die of old age, but of loneliness?

Yours,

Wendell

(By the way, your strawberry birthday cake was so good. I'm sorry I barely left any of it for you).

***

The day after her sad birthday, at exactly two o'clock in the afternoon, Deedee spotted Wendell's orange Mustang parked outside her home. He knew she'd be in, sitting, as she always did, at the desk in her bedroom, the turtle miniature placed in its left corner, and the white angel on the right. She had just finished reading—for the sixth or seventh time, she'd lost count—the note he'd written her the previous day, wondering how to respond.

As she sat there, Wendell stepped out of the car, walked over to the trunk, pulled out a blue suitcase, and placed it in the backseat. Then he walked to the window in the front of the house, knocked on it three times, and waited with a small yet meaningful smile on his face.

She opened the window carefully. "You're about to head out," she said, smiling curiously. "Where to?"

"I don't know," he said. His expression was that of typical Wendell-esque carelessness, but his eyes shone their little light at her. "Like the rabbit from *Alice in Wonderland* said, When you don't know which way to go, head north."

"That's not what he said," she countered.

"Oh, well, he must have said something

similar. It's been so long since I read the book, I can't remember anymore. You'll have to forgive me, Deedee."

They stood facing each other from both sides of the window for a few moments. Suddenly, he pulled out a small note and placed it against the windowpane, facing her. Deedee brought her face closer to the glass and began to read out loud: "Prescription for medication for the treatment of high cholesterol." Then she read out the long name of the drug, fighting to decipher the illegible handwriting. She looked at him imploringly.

"The gray repetitiveness of life here makes my cholesterol get out of whack," Wendell explained. "These small New Jersey towns can suffocate a guy without him even noticing. One day after the next, everything looking exactly the same, other than my face, which just keeps getting more wrinkles."

"But you... you only got back a few days

ago. And you're leaving already?"

"Only for a few days," he smiled. "I want to recall the New England landscape. I haven't traveled in this area in years."

Deedee stepped away from the window and back to her desk. She picked up the small note he'd left her the previous day. Turned it over and wrote on its other side: "Life in the suburbs of New Jersey does not cause high cholesterol. The unbridled eating of fatty cakes, however, does."

She held the note against the window and watched Wendell as he narrowed his eyes to read. When he finished, he glanced at her with a terribly severe look and she realized he did not like her direct sarcasm.

"Come in," she said. "I'll make us some tea. I was only joking."

"Thanks for the offer, but I'd rather get going," he said quietly.

She regretted what she'd written and was saddened to see him leave. She was surprised to discover she wanted him to stay. The moments they'd spent together the previous day were special, breaking her loneliness for a spell. Now she felt the disappointment nesting inside of her. *Why did he even come back, if he was only going to leave again?* She wondered. She forced out the words "Have a safe trip," then rose to her tiptoes and gave him a formal little hug. He was much taller than her and his shoulders were so narrow and hard she could feel his bones poking through. He wrapped his long, bony arms around her and leaned his head against her shoulder like a puppy. Surprised, Deedee held still, allowing him to embrace her. Finally, after what felt like an eternity, he let go and walked back to his car.

***

Deedee sighed. "Wendell, that weariless traveler," she mumbled to herself. Some people only enter your life for a short while, but once they are in it things are never the same again.

25

He was the kind of man she liked: his essence projecting nobility and serenity, while still maintaining a childish impishness. Most of all, she loved his wondrous ability to always be different than anyone else she knew, in a good way. His ability to live his life on his own without needing anyone else to make him whole impressed her to the point of pain. He had an inner discipline that she'd thought was preserved only for heroes. Years ago, whenever they met, a little jolliness crept into her heart, like a small, fluttering butterfly. And just like a butterfly, whose life ends all too quickly, only one year after they met, Wendell packed his belongings and left to go far away, to the other side of the planet, to start over in England. After he left, she found herself missing him. She hoped that because he was never her romantic partner his absence wouldn't leave too much of a mark, but she was surprised to find she'd been wrong.

She stood still in the large foyer for several minutes, staring at the decorated floor tiles. Then she went to the door and quickly opened it.

Wendell had already begun driving off when he saw her in the rearview mirror, running slowly out of her home, calling something to him. He rolled down his window and heard her shouting: "Wait! Wait, Wendell! Wait, I'm coming with you!"

His expression softened at once, a small smile sneaking its way onto his lips. He pulled up and rolled up the window. "I thought you'd never ask," he said sweetly as he opened the door for her.

"Let me pack a few things and I'll be right back," she said and went back inside. She slammed the door behind her, leaned against it, and listened carefully to her racing heart. "Dear God, what have I done?" She mumbled. Only now, pausing to think, she realized that at this point in her life she had no energy left for a trip whose purpose was not at all clear to her, let alone in the autumnal weather that had already begun chilling the air. Her legs hurt from chronic rheumatism and her mood was low. Just a few hours ago she wished to end her life, and now all she wanted to do was get back into her warm bed, read her library book about downtrodden women in Canada during World War II, have a cup of tea, and take an excessively long afternoon nap.

But it was too late. She'd already given her word to Wendell, and an inner force was pulling her toward the unknown against her better judgment. She was caught in the midst of inner turmoil, her heart asking for one thing while her brain fought for another, shooting its all-too familiar arrows of doubt and concern. How did she get here? She wondered. She'd only listened to her heart few times throughout her life, but this time she knew that against all logic, this was the right thing to do. Sometimes loneliness makes people do odd things, she thought with a smile. Then she took a deep breath and walked slowly into the small storage space. She pulled out a small silver trolley and wiped off the film of dust. This was Benjie's suitcase, which she'd never used. They married at age thirty and he became her anchor. Along with Alma and her sister, he was the only family she ever had. Then one morning, when he was seventy two years old, he rested his head on his desk, closed his eyes, and returned his soul to his maker. He was an introvert who spoke few words and parted with his life the same way he'd lived it: quietly, without any explanations.

But Deedee knew that people didn't just leave unwillingly. A higher being within us, her beloved spiritual books had taught her, chose to do so. She'd known Benjie long enough to sense he was simply too tired. He was a workhorse who spent many hours of his day on the job. After retirement he failed to find a new spice to his life. Until that moment he'd known himself through his work and his colleagues. When that was gone, it was as if his identity had been taken along with it.

In the days after his retirement he would watch her with sad eyes from behind the morning paper, wondering how to pass the long day ahead. She noticed the desperation that took hold of him, turning him into somebody else.

"How many years can a single pump keep working? Doesn't that little organ ever give up?" That is what he asked her mere days before he died. "So much blood streaming between four chambers for so many years. Go figure."

And eventually his heart did give in, and she knew that beneath this banter that emerged in the few words he said, dwelled a sad, heavy truth.

"If you don't suffer too much heartache," she answered him once, "I think it can go on beating for a long time."

"Who doesn't have heartache?" he quipped, not expecting an answer, his eyes continuing to flutter over the morning news.

Deep inside there were lots of things she

wanted to tell him but never dared. On the other hand, there were many things she did say which would have been better left unsaid. Benjie's death left her feeling guilty and remorseful, plagued by unresolved emotional complications that were never discussed. She loved him, but more than that, she was used to him, like a bird more familiar with its cage than with its ability to fly. The day she said goodbye to him for the last time her heart flinched at the sounds of the clumps of dirt hitting his coffin. That day at the cemetery she wailed like a baby, and continued to do so for days on end. The pain of parting was also accompanied by the pain for his life and hers, lives not fully lived; for their love that had persevered like a small wild flower alongside a field of weeds.

***

It was a convenient suitcase, the kind that required only a light touch and then seemed to glide ahead on its own. She carefully placed in it some of the neatly folded clothes in her closet:

two pairs of pants, two long-sleeved flannel shirts, two sweaters, and pajamas. Then she went up to the bathroom and packed her red toiletry bag with a toothbrush, moisturizer, dental floss, toothpaste, mouthwash, shampoo, cotton swabs, facial cleanser, body lotion, and calamine lotion. She went back downstairs and into the bedroom and added ten pairs of thick socks, a bottle of multivitamin pills, anti-constipation tea, heartburn medicine, and hypertension medicine.

She went back into the kitchen and glanced at the juicer on the counter, prominent and clunky on the backdrop of the smaller appliances around it. She considered it for a moment, then grabbed it and shoved it into a small black bag, ignoring its inordinate size. The ginger-lemon-veggie juice she had every morning for years was more important to her than all her medicine, and she decided it was worth lugging around. It was as if the juicer's presence could protect her from the great unknown of this trip, as if one glass of juice was enough to maintain her general health and sanity.

She was worried she might have still forgotten something, and sat down at the kitchen table, trying to recall if there was anything else she needed. After a while she got up and went to the central heating switch to make sure it was turned on low. Then she wandered the kitchen, checking and rechecking that the oven and stove were turned off, and only then, utterly exhausted, she walked outside, straight into a darkening November afternoon, and into Wendell Parker's old orange Mustang. In spite of her heavy heart and through her aching, fading legs, she knew it was time for a change. Throughout those years when things never changed on the outside, she remembered her grandfather quoting that famous saying: "Insanity is doing the same thing over and over again and expecting different results."

She slowly opened the door to the backseat of the overheated car and brought her suitcase inside. Wendell, who'd dozed off while waiting for her now opened his eyes and let out a long yawn. Then he got out of the car and helped her with her things.

"Sorry to keep you waiting," she said as she sat down in the passenger seat and buckled up.

Wendell smiled. He didn't mind waiting for almost an hour. Where did they have to rush off to? "So what do you say?" he asked. "Shall we hit the road?"

"Yes. But where should we go?"

"As the rabbit said to Alice, 'If you don't know where you are going any road can take you there.'

"Yes, that's exactly what he said. And if you recall, after that she got lost…"

Wendell's smile never faded. "That isn't necessarily a bad thing," he said. "You have to get lost before you can find your way again, don't you?"

***

Wendell's old Mustang rolled slowly down the street. Wendell preferred it to any new car. Its aging style reminded him of himself: rusty but still fit. Even the constant treatment of different motor parts was enjoyable to him.

They passed through trains of golden leaves hovering gracefully down the road. Wendell took in the sights around them. "Look at this gorgeous autumn," he said. "The trees seem to glow in colors that summer has never seen. Fall foliage. I love this season." His eyes shone. "There is beauty even in death," he said simply.

Deedee said nothing, pondering his words. Death meant so many things to her, but beauty had never been one of them. Benjie's head plopped on the desk, his arms hanging alongside his body in surrender—these did not look beautiful to her when she walked into his office and found him lifeless. As far as she was concerned, she was gazing into a black pit that had opened up in the earth before her very eyes. Mere minutes earlier he said he was hungry and she'd gone into the kitchen to make the two of them some breakfast. But when she went in to call him to the table he was no longer there.

"Death is too frightening for me to think of it as beautiful," she answered honestly. "Aren't you afraid... to die?" Her voice trembled a bit as she said that word, *die.*

"No."

"Why not?"

"Because when I die I'll no longer be me. I will have moved on." His expression told her he truly believed it. "The man I was at age thirty is long dead. I can't remember anything about him now. We are constantly transforming."

Enormous carpets of red and golden leaves covered the ground and the edges of the road, as if decorating the world in expectation of winter, moments before it froze over. They rode in silence, watching the houses and cars passing them by. A lively world began creeping into the small car, and from there straight into the gray spaces of Deedee's heart, coloring them with new impressions.

The sky slowly grew dim. "It isn't death you're afraid of," he said, "but uncertainty. Death is uncertainty." Wendell took a sip from his water bottle. He was growing tired of the drive and began looking around for a place to pull up.

"Actually," said Deedee, "death is completely certain. It's life that's uncertain." She looked at him and recalled all those deep conversations about life they used to have. It felt good, talking with him like this again. On the night they'd first met, too many years ago to count, there was an especially beautiful sunset. She hadn't noticed it, but he called her attention to the sun, which painted the clouds pink and gold upon its descent. They found themselves talking for a long time in that crowded park in a scorching late August. Finally, when she stood up to leave, he asked for her phone number.

The next time they met, it was in her small apartment. She couldn't find clothes that were flattering enough and had trouble fixing her hair. Finally, overcome with excitement, she ended up in the same plain outfit she'd worn all day long, and only had time to quickly pull up her mussed hair. She managed to light candles on the kitchen table and arrange it with a vase of small white roses she'd bought that morning. When the doorbell rang, her heart pounded with tentative joy, like a tiny goldfish meeting the deep sea for the very first time.

Just like on that first night, that evening they once again found themselves talking deep into the night. After that she didn't return his phone calls for a few days, as if wishing to linger a bit longer in that delight that is reserved for new beginnings, like savoring the taste of cake. Four days later, she called him back. She hoped with all her heart for a sign of courtship, something to move their relationship in a romantic direction. When this didn't happen, she had no choice but to accept their status as good friends and nothing more. They met often, going together to the movies and to restaurants. He seemed happy to be around her, loving her as a good friend. He never knew her true feelings for him.

Deedee took a deep breath and looked at the world raging outside, a world she'd nearly forgotten in the many hours she spent in her closed-off home. Wendell's little car merged onto the freeway and sped up. The trees and road signs began to flicker by quickly, and she glanced curiously at the names of small towns on both sides of the freeway, names she'd never heard before.

"While we're on the subject of death," Wendell said, breaking the silence, "people don't usually say this out loud, but at our age we could die at any given moment. At least now we've got plenty of free time to do the things we love. Young people are so busy all the time."

Deedee's eyes stayed fixed on the view. She

sighed deeply and nodded. The sun set, leaving behind it a dark gray November sky. Another day was over.

"I'm hungry," she said. "We should stop for some food."

They had been driving for some hours, and now it was dinner time. Two elderly people, unaware of how lucky they were to have reached their respectable ages with a mind as clear as it was years earlier, their speech eloquent, and their tired bodies still willing to obey their wishes.

"Good God, I'm hungry too. Look at the time!" said Wendell.

It was late at night by the time they found a place to sleep. They didn't know the name of the small town, only noticed that it was surrounded by thick maples and wide corn fields stretching on the sides of the road. The full moon made the sky look silver and somewhat artificial, as if they'd reached the edge of the world. The brown brick house had three stories. The owners lived on the first two floors, and rented out a modest room on the third floor.

Deedee got out first, stretched her arms and legs and sighed a loud relief. They had been driving for almost five hours without stopping, and her legs had stiffened so much that now she limped a little. In the end they hadn't even stopped for food. Outside the house was a small pond surrounded by thick bulrushes. She was cold. She crossed her arms against her body and looked up to the sky. The glowing moon looked back at her, indifferent to the chill and dark of the night. On the ancient oak tree standing sentinel on the edge of the pond perched a small black crow, cawing loudly.

"What kind of owl sounds like that?" Deedee asked, looking in the direction of the sound.

"Not an owl, a crow," Wendell corrected her. "When I was a kid there were lots of crows in my hometown. My father always said that the cawing crow was a symbol of the death of a loved one."

"I've never been a fan of those birds," she said, beginning to walk toward the house. Taking the stairs slowly, they went up to the room. Deedee gripped the banister, careful not to trip.

"I'll make us some tea and we can have some oatmeal cookies I bought this morning," said Wendell, filling a kettle with water and turning on the small electric stove in the corner of the room. "Lucky for us, we're old people who can make do with cookies for dinner."

"You've never been short on excuses for eating cookies and cakes," she said with a smile.

"That's because I've somehow managed to stay a child, and children love sweet foods," he said, returning her smile and shoving a large oatmeal chocolate chip cookie into his mouth. As he chewed, he closed his eyes with pleasure at the soft sweetness. The room was nice and cozy, and after gobbling down a few more cookies, Wendell announced he was going to the bathroom to wash up.

Deedee sat on the chair near the bed and watched the indifferent moon hanging in the enormous sky through the window. It was surrounded with a white aura that threw light all around it. "So far away, you and I," she whispered to it. "Both so small in this vast universe, surrounded by countless galaxies and planets and God knows what else. At least you don't know how great your lonesomeness is," she said sadly, sipping the hot, sweet tea, way too sweet for her taste. "And you know what else?" she turned to the moon again, her face adorned with a melancholic smile. "Being lonesome is a lot easier when you're young than when you're old."

***

"Wild horses couldn't drag me away... Wild, wild horses..."

Wendell was singing in the shower at the top of his lungs.

"I've got my freedom, but I don't have much

time…"

When he emerged his body smelled from the sweet rose-scented soap that must have been left by a previous guest. As he walked he dripped a long train of water on the old wooden floor. Before reaching the bed he dropped the towel and then crawled in, naked as the day he was born, burrowing into the thick comforter. Deedee got a glimpse of his narrow behind and his loose skin. "It feels so good to lie in bed naked," he said, closing his eyes, allowing the effort of the day to dissipate back into the night.

She stared at him awkwardly, and he seemed to read her mind. His eyes startled open as he said, "Oh, I'm so sorry, Deedee, I didn't mean to make you uncomfortable. I'm just so used to getting into bed naked right after taking a bath. I'll… I'll put some clothes on."

Realizing he was about to get out of bed, naked, she determined loudly: "No! No need! Stay there. The thought of having to see him nude again, this time from a front angle, terrified her. "I'll go to the bathroom and give you some privacy," she said, fleeing to the bathroom and closing the door behind her as quickly as she could.

"Hey, Deedee, come on, for God's sake, you don't think I'm trying to make a move on you, do you? It was just a force of habit."

"I didn't think that," she called out from beyond the bathroom door, sitting on the closed toilet lid. She stayed put for some time, wondering how she'd even gotten there—to that town, to that bizarre trip with a man for whom she'd always felt an intense affection, but whom she hadn't seen in decades until just yesterday.

***

"What kind of name is Wendell, anyway?" she asked him one of the first times they'd met. He was still living with his mother, and that was where they'd met that day. As she walked into the house she could immediately feel the gloom of the large living room. The furniture was arranged carefully and it seemed like a long time since it had last been used. His mother emerged from the kitchen, carrying a large towel, offered her hand, and gave Deedee a long look.

"This is Deedee," Wendell said quietly. Then he took Deedee's hand and led her to the large porch overlooking a vast field yellowing with summer.

His features resembled his mother's: a slightly bumpy nose and sunken dark eyes. Deedee noticed that same twinkle in his mother's eyes, a kind of flash of constant cheer diluted with sorrow. "I'll leave you two alone," said the mother, disappearing into the distant kitchen. She was a pretty woman, her short dark hair framing her face nobly and her general demeanor projecting an unusual combination of strength and fragility.

"You have a beautiful home," said Deedee.

"Thanks," said Wendell. "I used to like it

better. It got too big for me after my father died."

"Oh, I'm so sorry… I didn't know."

"Yes, two years ago. A heart attack at age fifty-two."

"Do you have any siblings?"

"No, it's only me and my mother."

Not wanting to talk any further about his father, he stood up and went into the kitchen. When he returned he poured both of them some sweet tea from a white china pot. She sipped the hot beverage, savoring its flavor. It was the first time a man had invited her over to his home, and she felt as if a woman who had been dwelling anonymously inside of her had suddenly come to life.

"Your mother must be sad to see you go."

"Yes, very sad," he answered drily, looking out onto the field. "I know that by the act of going away I'm hurting her, but it's better for her if I'm far away. I worry about her too much, it isn't healthy for either of us."

"Did she choose your name?"

"No," he said with a small smile. "My father did. I never liked the name. It's archaic, don't you think? It means wanderer. He named me after his father, who had also died young. They don't last too long, the Parker men." Wendell's face darkened. "He was a hard man," he added. "He didn't like anyone in this world other than the two of us, but even with us he was too stern."

"It's a nice name, Wendell," she said quietly, embarrassed by his sudden sincerity. Then she glanced at her watch and said urgently that she had to go, though she truly wanted to stay. It had been exactly an hour since her arrival, and manners dictated that she must leave.

On her way home, walking briskly down the gray sidewalk, she felt a cool breeze penetrating through her thin jacket and a familiar sadness tickling up her throat. *Wendell the wanderer,* she thought. *I wish you didn't have to go.*

***

A long time later she finally emerged from the bathroom and looked at him wordlessly.

"Why are you looking at me like that?"

"Like what?"

"Like I'm a dirty old man."

"Maybe because you are."

"Then you do think I was making a move on you." He was speaking too loudly for her taste. His hearing wasn't great. She'd already noticed that the previous day.

"I think it's been a very long time since I've spent longer than an hour with anyone," she said gravely. "It isn't easy for me, being around other people."

Wendell sat beside her on the bed. He was wearing a red plaid flannel shirt and wide jeans that made him look young and cozy. Since he always slept in the nude he didn't have any pajamas. While Deedee was in the bathroom he quickly put on his clothes again.

"I'll sleep on the rug," he said decisively, walking to the wooden closet near the door and pulling out a blanket.

Deedee slipped into bed, lying on her back. "It's fine, you can sleep in bed," she said quietly. She knew he meant it, but didn't feel comfortable letting him sleep on the floor all night long.

Wendell slipped back into the double bed and lay flush against the wall on the other side, careful not to touch her. She covered both of them with the thick comforter. Now they were both lying on their backs, watching the high ceiling, listening to the silence. It was a different silence than the one she was used to hearing each night as she tossed and turned in her large bed, trying and failing to shut out the sad, compulsive thoughts that raced through her mind.

She'd forgotten how much desire still existed in her old body. How she yearned for a touch, an embrace. She took Wendell's hand in hers and closed her eyes, feeling a cloud of soft cotton caressing her.

"Good night," said Wendell sleepily and melted into his sleep. His body rose and fell under the comforter to the monotonous beat of his snoring.

She lay beside him for a long time, unable to fall asleep. Was she homesick, or perhaps yearning for Alma, her daughter, whom she hadn't seen in almost a year? "Yearning is just another thought," she mumbled to herself, tired, and then sank into a deep sleep as well.

***

Morning. The first rays of sun filtered through the large windows, hitting her face with bright, white light. Deedee's eyes opened at once and she looked at the clock on the bedside table. It was ten past six. She sat on the edge of the bed, squinting at the light. She slowly looked over the small, quiet room, but found no sign of Wendell. When she went to the bathroom to wash her face, she saw his toothbrush on the edge of the sink, surrounded by toothpaste marks. She used some of the toothpaste that was resting on the small shelf and was surprised by the strong cinnamon flavor, so different than what she was used to. She got dressed, put on her white sneakers, and took the stairs down slowly, wondering where he could have run off too so early in the morning.

Outside, she was met by the new, fresh scent of morning. In spite of the early hour she felt completely alert. She breathed in the sour smell of weeds wet with dew. A small butterfly fluttered by, searching for nectar in the small wild flowers of the field. She strolled around, listening to the humming of small insects flying and hopping all around. It had been so long since she'd been in nature, she couldn't even remember the last time. She took a seat on a small wooden bench and watched the swampy pond whose water was green and murky. It had been too dark the previous night to notice its beauty.

She was looking around for Wendell when she thought she saw something swimming in the water. She squinted and walked over to the edge of the pond, trying to decipher what her eyes saw. The sun blinded her and she shielded her eyes with her hand, when she saw Wendell floating on his stomach, completely still, his face underwater, and his arms spread beside him lifelessly. Her blood dropped down to her feet, planting them in the ground until they felt paralyzed. She didn't know what to do. Should she run—as much as she could run—back into the house to call for help? Or should she dive in and try to rescue him on her own? Would she be able to? She wasn't sure...

A jumble of thoughts bounced through her mind so fast that she felt faint and collapsed back down onto the bench, staring helplessly as Wendell floated motionlessly in the greenish water.

Suddenly, Wendell opened his eyes, tipped over and stood up in the water, taking a deep breath in and sighing a loud breath out. He whooped as he wiped his wet face with his hands. "At my age it's not so simple to hold your breath for that long!"

"Good grief, Wendell, you've been holding your breath this whole time? Why did you do that? You gave me a hell of a scare." Deedee's face was ashen.

It was just like that time, years ago, when he decided to go travel alone in a large forest with only a tent, a sleeping bag, and a few cans of corn and chickpeas. He invited her to join him, but sleeping out in nature with bears and other beasts roaming freely was too frightening to her. When he returned, five days later, and knocked on her door at twilight, his skin burned from the sun, she felt a great sense of relief, surprised to find just how much she'd worried about him.

***

Wendell wiped away the water that still streamed down his face and looked at her, embarrassed. "I didn't think you'd come down here so early. I was sure I was alone and I was curious to know how long I could hold my breath for. You know, I used to be able to go three whole minutes!" Wendell swam toward her. When he reached the shore he put his hands on the ground and pushed down until he was finally able to pull himself out of the water, revealing his naked body to her again. Looking away, she threw over his long raincoat, which had been lying on the bench.

Wendell wrapped the coat around his body and sat down beside her, dripping water. His feet were muddy.

"I thought you were dead," she said, looking at him gravely.

"I'm sorry. I didn't mean to scare you."

"The water is so cold, how did you even get

yourself in there?" She was feeling the blood flowing down her legs once again.

"It felt wonderful. The water was freezing so I had to swim fast to get warm. I could feel life beating inside me in full force. All my old cells came to life."

She looked over at the pond. "You could have drowned," she said, her voice hard." And you almost gave me a heart attack... That's irresponsible." Deedee felt the wave of concern for his safety transforming at once into boiling anger. "I don't know what I was thinking, going on a trip with an old devil like you." She got up and began limping back toward the brick house across the field. "Why did you have to just show up like that?" she muttered, turning around to give him a cold look that stopped him in his tracks. "You and your foolish whims!"

Wendell watched her walk away. His coat was drenched. He was shivering. "Deedee, wait, don't go," he called after her. I'm sorry.

She walked on, not looking back until she disappeared into the house. When she got to the room she lay down on the bed and broke into tears.

Wendell walked into the room and straight into the bathroom, where he dried himself off. When he came out, he sat down on the edge of the bed and looked at her with sad eyes. "I'm going to have to get used to traveling with a companion," he said quietly. "You know, I've grown so used over the years to going it alone. I truly didn't imagine you'd come outside so early."

She nodded. Crying had worn her out. she was no longer mad, only uncomfortable for having invaded another's territory. "And I'll have to get used to seeing your wrinkled rear-end from time to time," she answered, her eyes puffy.

He smiled wide.

"You've always been adventurous, the exact opposite of me. I've only ever searched for familiar anchors."

They sat silently for a while. For the first time since they'd set off, Wendell's serene face became cracked with sorrow. His eyes wandered beyond the window to a small red breasted bird hopping lightly across the green meadow. "I don't remember if I ever told you I have a son, Josh. A son I've barely raised. I left home right after he was born. It was a shotgun wedding, a fast infatuation that died out. It was probably my single attempt to live like everybody else. We were together for a year, and then we couldn't do it anymore." His face was serious. He folded his arms over his body like a turtle burrowing into its shell, and stared at the horizon. "The last time I saw him was four years ago, the last time I was in New Jersey. I've been through so much in the time I haven't seen you, Deedee. I wish you knew…"

***

A 1969 faded orange Mustang rolls slowly down long, seemingly endless winding roads that appear to be leading nowhere, twisting and turning across the vast American continent. They could drive for many years and never see its myriad sights.

There, inside that car, are two people who, in spite of the troubles they'd lived through, have made it to a very respectable age indeed, an age to beat all ages.

They'd been driving for over two hours, passing by godforsaken towns, crossing the state of New York, passing by Massachusetts and New Hampshire in their aimless ride toward Canada. All the small places on the side of the road looked the same to her. She wondered if the people who lived in them all felt the same loneliness, a sense of a life not fully lived. Did the days all look the same to them too? Did time pass by too quickly for them, leaving them ensconced in their defeat? She pulled a green apple from her bag and bit into it. Its tart flavor was more delicious than ever. Suddenly, there, in a car with a man she hadn't seen in years, riding through strange roads and thick, centuries-old maple trees, each bite of the apple was accompanied by an odd desire to return to life. To live.

Morning evaporated slowly and faded into a sleepy afternoon. Deedee closed her eyes and leaned her head back. The car was so quiet she could hear her own breathing.

"My toenails have turned hard and yellow," Wendell suddenly said.

Deedee opened her eyes.

"I cheer myself up by telling myself that it's better than losing my teeth. Luckily, I still have all of my trusty teeth with me."

She smiled awkwardly. "Oh, yes, my toenails have gone yellow long ago," she said. "I think I noticed it when I was seventy, or a bit later." She tried, unsuccessfully, to recall the exact timing.

They rode on, time melting beneath their hands like a popsicle on a hot summer day. For Deedee, going on this trip was like leaving a fortified castle straight into the bustle of a crowded marketplace. She'd never imagined that life dwelled between those moments of uncertainty. She was tired and hoped they'd arrive somewhere, unsure whether to feel happy or sad about the distance between her and her little home and garden. A part of her was glad for being exactly here, in Wendell's little car, in the middle of nowhere. After years of loneliness, she now had a living, breathing being to speak to.

"It's been a long day," she said. Her feet were frozen and her body tight from the prolonged sitting. She hadn't eaten in hours and was beginning to feel grumpy.

"Being preoccupied with one's self makes one indifferent to the beauty of the universe," he teased her.

"I just need my home back," she answered quietly, her eyes growing moist. She needed to use the bathroom, but how could she explain to him that at her age crouching over a public toilet bowl was impossible? Suddenly, she wanted her mother by her side, embracing her with her familiar, bony arms. She yearned to feel that strong grip again, a suffocating hug after which she always had to take a deep breath to recover, and which, nevertheless, she now missed. After all, it was the first hug she'd ever known.

Eventually, in the late afternoon, exhausted after a long day of driving, they stopped at a small bed and breakfast. Wendell popped the trunk and Deedee dragged out her suitcase, insisting on carrying it up the narrow flight of stairs herself. She moved slowly, one step after the other, the suitcase grating against the old wood. When she arrived in their bedroom she pulled out her large, cumbersome juicer.

Wendell took a seat on the bed and watched her with amusement. He was tired and wanted nothing more than to take a shower and go to sleep. He watched as she fished through her bag and pulled out a bag of lettuce and cabbage leaves, three cucumbers, and a bundle of kale.

Then she brought out a lemon, sliced it, and put everything into the maw of the juicer.

"You're going to make juice now?" he asked. It's 11:20 at night."

"I absolutely am," she said roughly. "I need this juice right now. I only wish I hadn't already eaten my apple, I could have used it."

Wendell said nothing, cringing at the ruckus made by the juicer, like a laundry machine wringing out clothes. When she was finished, Deedee poured the juice into two paper cups she had brought with her, then wiped off the green trail that had dripped across the table. She offered one cup to Wendell and then sat down on the bed and gulped down her juice, her face serene. Wendell tried to disguise his distaste for the bitterness of the green juice. "You have to add the apples next time," he said, standing up and going to the bathroom to take a shower and put an end to this long day.

"Yes, it's bitter this way," she called out from

behind the closed door. "Bitter, but healthy."

"If it only tasted like coffee I'd drink it every day," he called back to her before stepping under the showerhead and closing his eyes.

***

The next morning they got up early and without a word continued their strange journey down the open road. She wanted to ask him where they were headed, but didn't. She was surprised to find how quickly she was adapting to a life of wandering. The radio played the harmonious sounds

of a guitar, and the winding turns rocked her with their own unique tempo.

"It's very bright today," she said, looking out the window. It looked like a summer day outside, making it easy to forget how cold it actually was. "My sister used to call it a false sun." She sighed, feeling the familiar discomfort that always came up whenever she thought about Rosie. "I haven't talked to her in months," she said. "She and I, just like the sun, are false sisters." After a brief pause, she added: "I suppose the distance between our towns and the fact that we're both old ladies who don't get out much hasn't helped."

Rosie was Deedee's older sister. She was the one who watched her during the long evenings when their parents had to work, lifting Deedee up in her arms so she could reach the light switch. Ever since she was a little girl, Deedee carried shards of memories of the two of them. She remembered the way they used to curl up together in Rosie's bed, where Rosie told her a made-up story about a little dwarf that no one but them could see. Deedee would crawl under the covers, searching for the dwarf, while Rosie tickled her feet. They loved each other dearly, but eventually each chose to live her life alone, far away from each other both physically and emotionally. In this kind of reality even a great love is not enough.

"Hey, Wendell, why don't we change

directions?"

"What do you mean?"

"How about we go visit Rosie?" she asked hesitantly, as if still pondering her own proposal. It had been six years since they'd last seen each other and four months since they'd last spoken. The truth was, she didn't think they would ever see each other again. Rosie was eighty-two years old, tired and ill, and neither of them was willing to put in the required effort to see the other. Or, perhaps it would be more accurate to say neither of them was willing to put in the effort required in opening their hearts to each other again. "She lives in Sullivan, Maine," Deedee said, looking out the window.

"You haven't seen each other in six years?" Wendell asked. "That's a long time." He looked ponderous. "Maine... I haven't been there in ages. It's at least a seven hour drive."

She nodded in agreement.

He smiled. "Why not? Let's go."

His almost instant consent filled Deedee with mixed emotions, her excitement diluted once again with an all too familiar distress. "It's been so many years," she whispered, "that now each renewed encounter might bring more pain than joy."

"It's painful, but it's still important, isn't it?" he asked, trying to brighten her mood. "Just like your green juice—bitter, but healthy."

***

Ithaca is a beautiful town, dotted by a lake, sailboats floating along it slowly, affording it a sleepy, picturesque look. Many artists and writers live there, as well as "regular" people who chose to get away from the hustle and bustle of the world, and who make a daily effort to find the point of their being there.

It had been many hours before they finally reached Ithaca late in the afternoon. They would go get a bite to eat, take a little stroll around town, then shift their northbound journey and go another direction, to Maine, to visit Rosie.

Better late than never, Deedee tried to reassure herself about her impulsive decision, hoping with all her heart that it wasn't later than she'd thought. She dragged her feet after Wendell, feeling a sharp pain in her hips with each step she took.

Wendell looked at her, realizing they'd spent too many hours in the car, He remembered how she used to go with him to the lake that was an hour away from the small town where Deedee still lived to this day. It took him an entire week to convince her to join him. Finally, tired of listening to his preaching, she agreed to join him for a weekend at the lake. He recalled the two of them sitting in an old fishing boat, Deedee insisting on rowing herself, gripping the heavy oars, her face red with effort, but happy to be surrounded by the clear water. The whole time she rowed she spoke to him with an almost unstoppable flow of words. Whenever they passed anything that looked remarkable to her— the fins of a fish or a colorful bird flying overhead—she was filled with sudden excitement, her face beaming.

"I knew you'd end up thanking me for this trip," he'd told her and she smiled, aware of the fact that he'd given her an unforgettable weekend. *Things have changed a bit,* he thought, feeling a tug at his heart strings at the sight of her slow movements and strained face.

"I'm tired," she said, taking a seat on a park bench.

Wendell paused, took a few steps back, dropped his large backpack onto the ground and took a seat next to her. He was wearing tall hiking boots and looked for a moment like a man in his twenties on his way to a trek. When he bought them, he thought that even though he wasn't about to go mountain climbing he still preferred to wear shoes intended for that kind of activity.

He liked knowing they could handle long nature walks. "Deedee," he said, "if you've had enough we don't have to go all the way to Maine. We can always go home, all right?"

"I don't know. Maybe we can stay here for the night and keep going tomorrow?"

"Yes, we'll keep going tomorrow." He put his palm over her hand, gave it a pat and smiled at her. "After all, we're not in any kind of rush."

She smiled back at him. "Remember that train we never made? We got to the station just in time to see it pulling away."

"Yes… and you ran ahead and yelled at me to run too. My boots got covered in mud."

"I remember. I wanted to make it so badly."

"We ended up taking the bus instead, two hours longer."

"Yes… and on the way you ate a sandwich that made the entire bus stink of onions. I remember it like it was yesterday."

"I don't remember that part. But you're probably right. I still love onions."

Deedee's eyes sparkled. For a moment she thought her vision was getting blurry. She was a little dizzy. "Benjie didn't eat onions or garlic," she said suddenly. "He liked delicate flavors."

"Do you think about him a lot?" he asked quietly.

"Not at all," she said decisively. "I'm often surprised at how much time goes by without my remembering him. And still… I do miss him. A lot. Come on, let's keep going," she said, getting up and making an effort to walk in a straight line down the stone path. The sun had long since set, and a street light illuminated the twisting paths softly. She wrapped her jacket around her body, protecting herself from the strong wind that made it rain with leaves, which then piled heavily on the ground. She watched the naked trees, looking somewhat sad, and new thoughts began sneaking into her head, thoughts of a kind she'd never had before. If Wendell hadn't left when he did, would they have become romantic partners? If they had, what chance would she have had at making it with a man who loved his freedom more than anything? Would she have been happy with him, or just as lonely as she'd been all those years with Benjie? Her advanced age and the many years gone by left her full of questions and regrets for things that could have gone differently. She wanted to go back home, hide from the world again.

After they left the park they sat down in a small café that smelled pleasantly of soup and warm sandwiches. Wendell ordered a bowl of soup and when it arrived he began to eat it with fervor, not waiting for it to cool first. The flavor of sweet potatoes reminded him of being a child. He was feeling cold from the long walk and the soup seemed to have thawed him. He felt neither happy not sad, but just like a man who had paused for a few moments in the middle of a journey to no place in particular. Deedee debated between the different menu items, struggling to find something that reminded her of home. Eventually, she settled on a large bowl of oatmeal with raisins.

"We're eating the kind of food people have after they've suffered a stroke," he joked, "but it tastes pretty damn good." After finishing his soup, Wendell ordered two slices of pecan pie and two cups of tea. *I'm sitting here, with a lady I barely know, listening to the bustling sounds of an evening café*, he thought to himself, amused, as he sipped his tea. She looked at him affectionately, making him feel better than he had in years. These were the small, crucial things that had been missing from his life in so long. He began to feel an intimacy with her that he hoped she shared, but was simultaneously concerned about her ability to carry on with this trip.

By the time they finished their dinner it was late and as they stepped outside they were greeted by a cold rush of air. Curled into her heavy jacket, she dragged behind him toward the wooden cabin where they were to spend the night. She had no idea why she'd agreed to spend the night in the middle of nature, but now it was too late to change her mind. The cabin was located in a small forest and contained a single bed with metal frames and a tiny bathtub. She sat beside him outside the cabin near the fire he'd started, and after thirty minutes grew too cold and went inside to prepare for a night in the narrow bed, hoping she'd be able to find a position comfortable enough for her aching body. Outside she heard Wendell singing quietly to himself. He was roasting marshmallows on a branch, a little tipsy from the beer he'd had earlier. Suddenly, she heard a rustle inside the darkness of the room. She looked around her for the source of the sound, lying still for several moments on her back. Was she imagining it? But no, the sound continued. She cried out: "Wendell! Wendell!!!"

Wendell jumped to his feet and hurried into the cabin.

"There's someone in here," she whispered. "I heard something moving. Could it be a fox?" Her heart was pounding, her body growing petrified beneath the blanket.

Wendell ran his eyes over the dark room but couldn't see anything unusual. There were sticky residues of white marshmallow around his lips and he looked more ridiculous to her than ever before. "I don't hear anything," he said quietly. At that moment, the silence was broken by a long meow. Wendell looked toward the sound, which came from the small kitchenette, and spotted a large red cat standing in the corner, its back arched and its tail pointed. Surprised, Wendell walked over carefully, leaned down, and pet the soft fur, reassuring the animal.

"How did this cat get in here?" Deedee asked, sitting up in bed, staring at the furry creature with relief. "Maybe it smelled us and came to beg for food," she offered.

With the cat following assertively and

rubbing up against his coat, Wendell went into the kitchen, where he offered the cat the leftover corn from dinner. The cat gobbled it up. "Oh," Wendell mumbled softly, "Josh would have loved you. That kid loves animals."

Wendell turned away from the cat and spread his thick sleeping bag at the foot of Deedee's bed. He let out a loud sigh of relief when he finally lay down on his back. The cat climbed on top of him, licking Wendell's fingertips, which were still sticky with marshmallow, before sprawling out along the man's warm belly, closing its eyes, and falling asleep. Wendell fell asleep too within moments, and snored louder and deeper with each breath. The cat's purrs and Wendell's snores created a symphony of two wanderers who had crossed each other's path on a cold night under the moon.

Deedee lay back down on the hard, narrow mattress, trying to decide if the image of the two of them was funny or sad. For a long time she tossed and turned in the dark, watching the silhouettes at her feet, wondering how it could be that here, on a narrow bed with an unbearably hard mattress, so far away from home, for the first time in years, she did not feel alone.

The next morning she picked up the cell phone she hardly ever used and tapped in Rosie's phone number with trembling fingers. Deedee assumed Rosie would be awake at this early hour, as old ladies are wont to. She listened to the ringing, expectant of her sister's familiar, businesslike tone on the other end. But the ringing went on and on. When Rosie didn't answer, Deedee hung up and called again, but again nobody picked up.

Wendell was still lying on his back in the sleeping bag, solving a crossword puzzle.

"I'll try again in a little while," said Deedee, peeking out through the narrow window. "It's so cold outside. Seems like it might start snowing soon. Should we get going?"

Wendell got up slowly, pulled out his toothbrush and red cinnamon toothpaste, went to the small kitchen sink, and quickly brushed his teeth. When he finished, he rinsed his mouth with water from a bottle and spat it back into the sink. "Yes, I suppose we could hit the road," he said matter-of-factly and began to pack up.

Deedee, who had awoken long before he had, was already packed. She placed her small suitcase outside the door and began walking quietly toward the car, hoping that once they started going again the little lump in her throat would evaporate.

Before they left, Wendell looked around for his furry companion to say goodbye, but the cat was nowhere to be found.

WINTER

When people have nothing to say they speak mostly about unimportant things, but when they ought to say what is in their hearts, more often than not they opt for silence.

They had a long way to drive to Rosie's house. They began their journey, wondering whether they were making the right decision.

Wendell thought there was something off about the steering, as if something was tuck in the wheels, disrupting the car's motion. He wrote the sensation off as a result of the frozen road and kept going as usual. Before they'd taken off, he'd bought himself a cup of steaming coffee, which he now sipped slowly, hoping it might evaporate some of the fatigue he felt that morning.

Deedee chewed her apple languorously, enjoying its tartness.

"We could prolong life expectancy if only we found a way to make apples taste like cake," he said, then turned on the radio. Cheerful violin sounds filled the warm car.

"Pull over," Deedee suddenly cried. "Hurry!"

Surprised, Wendell came to a screeching stop at the side of the road. Deedee opened the car door and stepped outside wordlessly. She walked to the beach that was revealed to them, going all the way to the water. Her feet dug deep into the wet sand. All at once she leaned forward and began to throw up.

Once her body was emptied, she dropped to the ground, exhausted, and breathed in the salty ocean air. The sky was gray and full of heavy clouds that hid the sun and made the water appear black and gloomy. The cold smell of a winter wind invaded her nostrils, making her tired heart ache with loneliness. There was so much pain there. When she felt she couldn't contain the emotion another moment, she let out a scream so loud it reached all the way to the faraway indifferent sky. In response, a few seagulls that had been gliding elegantly now changed directions, flying away. Spent, she lay down on her back, feeling the pebbles piercing her skin, digging her hands deep into the sand.

Wendell lay down on the sand beside her. He looked

up at the flock of seagulls that had returned to circle the sky above their heads, sounding loud squawks. He held her hand tightly. They remained like this for several moments, lying wordlessly on the soft sand. His hand was warm and soft in spite of the cold and she felt his grip beyond the sand that covered her skin. They didn't care about the time. It could have been an hour or an entire afternoon, looking up silently at the ever-changing clouds, listening to the breaking waves touching the shore and retreating.

By the time they got up to head back to the car, the sun was already setting in the west. It was as if God's light itself was illuminating the world with golden grace. Soon, it would be night, and people's pain would gather in the darkness into the large, merciful womb of creation.

They got back into the warm car. The engine groaned and breathed in an effort to warm up. At their age, death was no longer a dramatic event, suppressed in the burrows of the heart. For the elderly, death is a daily companion, its smell felt deeply in their midst, like an innocent child taking in the wet scent of the air after rainfall.

Wendell looked worriedly at Deedee's frighteningly pale face. He noticed that something about her expression had changed. She was more peaceful than he'd ever seen her before.

The more they drove, the more she forgot all about death, which had been clawing at her like a persistent kitten. It was a blessed relief. After years of dying countless deaths in her dreams, she realized that these fantasies may be more frightening than the thing itself.

They stopped to look for a place to spend the night in a small town in Maine. In the parking lot of a small motel off the highway, a young man wearing a baseball cap watched them suspiciously from behind the wheel of a truck. "Sir," he called out to Wendell, who didn't hear him, continuing to pull the bags out of the car. His hearing was bad, and the loud rumble of the man's truck muffled the sounds altogether.

"Sir," the young man tried again, louder this time.

Wendell, who finally noticed him, looked over imploringly.

"Did you see what's sticking from your front bumper, sir?" the man asked.

Wendell walked over to the front of the car, looked

down at the bottom of the bumper, and was shocked to find a cat's legs dangling lifeless like a pair of old sneakers. "Dear God," Wendell cried, watching the dead cat hanging between the engine and the front of the car. He recognized his companion from the previous night instantly. At some point the cat must have wandered outside and found a bed for the night inside the warm engine. It did not manage to get out in time before Wendell and Deedee drove off that early morning. "Dear God," Wendell said again, cupping his cheeks in his hands. "I don't know what to say…" Appalled to his core he stared at the revolting vision. A tear pooled in the corner of his eye. "All day long I could feel the car wasn't running smoothly, but I didn't make anything of it," he said, perhaps to the young man, perhaps to himself.

Deedee walked over to the car and looked at the poor cat's body, appalled. Its mouth was half open and its eyes were closed. "How do we get it out of here?" she asked quietly.

The young man stepped out of his truck and around to the bed, where he pulled out a large garbage bag and a pair of grease stained work gloves. "I suppose we've just got to pull hard," he answered matter-of-factly. He realized that, unexcited though he was to touch the thing, he had no choice but to help out these two tired elders. He couldn't very well leave them out there with a dead cat dangling from their car.

***

When they finally entered their motel room late in the evening, Deedee crawled into bed in her clothes and unbraided her long hair. "I'll just take a little nap," she said quietly and sank heavily into the thick mattress.

Wendell sat down in a brown plush chair that had seen better days and watched her eyes retreat into their sockets. "Such heartache," he mumbled to himself. "Awful." Once she was asleep, he allowed himself to cry silently. The tears ran from his eyes as he tried not to think too much about the dead cat. His thoughts traveled to Josh, whom he hadn't seen in a long time. *He must be reading his little boy a bedtime story right now*, thought Wendell, picturing three-year-old James's angelic face. The last time they'd met, Wendell had given him a rubber hedgehog. The boy dipped the animal in paint and rolled it over a piece of paper like a brush, creating big, colorful shapes. Wendell hung the pictures by his bed and liked to look at them every night before he fell asleep.

"Go to sleep, Wendell, tomorrow's a new day." Deedee's voice, mumbling to him, half asleep, broke his reveries.

He got up from the chair and walked over to the bed. "I'd hoped that by now I'd understand a thing or two about this world," he said quietly, wiping his eyes. "But when things finally begin to look good, a dead cat comes along to make me realize I have no idea what's going on."

***

Early the next morning, Deedee woke up and changed into the last clean outfit she'd packed. She fixed her hair in a careful bun, making her look noble and elegant. Sleep had revived her. She went over to the car and paused by Wendell, who was staring at his front bumper.

"I killed a cat," he told her darkly, as if forgetting she'd been with him when it happened. She came closer and put her small hand on his shoulder. "But I pet him a lot the night before, and I think he was happy." Wendell sighed lengthily and slowly got into the car, his body more bent than usual. Deedee took her seat next to him and opened the glove compartment to put her wool cap inside. Suddenly, she let out a loud scream, slammed the glove compartment shut, and bolted out of the car.

Startled, Wendell followed her with imploring eyes. Her face was pale. "I think there's a dead mouse in the glove compartment," she said. Wendell's face twisted with revulsion and he walked hesitantly to the glove compartment, lingering before it. Then he forced himself to open it, expecting to see an awful sight. But then he took hold of the dead mouse and came out of the car, overcome with laughter. Deedee came closer to examine the small carcass, and was surprised to found it was nothing more than the rotten and molding core of an apple. The tension at the edges of her mouth made its way for her first smile since that morning.

"Oh," she said shyly, her voice drenched with relief. "Look at the stem," she said, pointing at the edge of the core. "It looks just like a mouse's tail. Simple mistake... I was so certain." Then she remembered she was the one who'd left the core in the glove compartment a few days ago and began to laugh as well.

***

The first snowflakes of the season began to fall, melting as they hit the tarmac. Deedee tried calling Rosie again, but again got no answer. She looked out the car window, hoping she'd get a hold of her before they arrived.

They were both lost in thought, so much so that Wendell hadn't even noticed he'd driven over three hours without stopping. Once he realized this, he began feeling fatigued, and so when he spotted the entrance to a sprawling state park he slowed down. This was the perfect place to stop: the park overlooked a lake dotted with tiny picturesque islands. It was already late afternoon when he stretched out his legs on a wooden bench. Deedee sat down beside him and watched the small sailboats that floated effortlessly across the water, relying on the wind to lead the way.

"Look at this perfect spot I found for you, Mrs. Deedee Field," he said, his voice tired. "Better than staying in and eating oatmeal alone in front of the television every morning."

"Actually, I miss my breakfast," she quipped, somewhat insulted by his critical tone.

"Sailboats floating across a lake for breakfast, full moon and owl hoots for dinner. That's the stuff of life," he said, staring at the water. The incident with the cat seemed to have brought out a painful darkness in him. She said nothing, hoping he would return to his graceful good spirits soon.

Suddenly they spotted a wooden shed containing long rows of bicycles for rent. Wendell's eyes widened and without thinking, like a child, he began to walk toward the small cabin. "It's been so long since I last rode a bike. I'm going to try again," he said. Before Deedee could reply he was already calling out from a distance: "I'll just go for a little spin and then we can go eat something." It was as if he'd never been tired.

Deedee remained alone on the bench, watching the people passing by. Soon, when she and Rosie finally meet again, she'd pull out the notebook filled with the poems she'd written for years and let her read it. She missed her sister's big brown eyes and was unsettled by the realization that Rosie's face was growing blurry in her memory. All of a sudden, she saw Wendell riding a bicycle down the path, in her direction, his body leaned forward on the silver sports bike, the helmet on his head making him look a little ridiculous.

He rode carefully, his eyes fixed on the path ahead,

his feet pedaling slowly. He wondered if she was watching, glad for the opportunity to impress her. Deedee waved hello and Wendell released one hand to wave back. He looked at Deedee and did not notice a small patch of ice right in the middle of the path. Had he seen it, he could have swerved, but he rode right over it, and his bicycle began wobbling, making him lose his balance. Worse still, it was a downhill path, and Wendell's attempts to brake all failed. Finally, he was flung off of the seat and landed against the hard stone pavement.

***

People have so many hopes and dreams throughout their lives, but in the end all that's left is memories. Among the shattered hopes and unfulfilled dreams, the image of her sister remained etched deep in Deedee's memory. She was the only one who'd shared her mother's womb with her, as well as the hard, twisting road of childhood. Their mother loved them in her own way, which often felt like anything but love. She was a holocaust survivor who diminished before their eyes year after year, trapped in her painful memories. Deedee knew how to take care of herself, escaping into the imaginary world of angels and fairies. Meanwhile, Rosie assumed the burden and took care of their mother. But when she was twenty-five Rosie finally gave up and moved away from the family. She, who never got the chance to truly be a child, now could not find the emotional resources to marry and start a family of her own. She was a painter and an art teacher, and a regular routine was her source of strength. The gray, indistinguishable days were her one true anchor.

***

Wendell couldn't remember the last time he fell this hard, and at such a special moment, to boot. He opened his eyes and looked at the bright walls. The last light of day filtered in through the windows. He tried to move his hands and felt a shooting pain and a hard cast along his right arm, affixing it in place.

"Older people fall a lot, we see it all the time," he heard a young man say above him.

"It isn't because of my age," he told the young doctor angrily as the man took his blood pressure. "I'm in great shape. It was just bad luck. I slipped on some ice…"

The doctor nodded with disinterest. "Stay in bed,

please. Someone will be in shortly to take you to get an X-ray."

"I can walk," Wendell said and tried to sit up, but then lay back down, surrendering. He wondered where Deedee was.

After the ambulance took Wendell away she sat back down on the bench, buttoned up her coat, and put on her woolen cap. She watched the ambulance drive away, having chosen not to get inside. She was paralyzed with panic. *I'll get up soon*, she told herself. There's still some light. I'll find my way out of this park and hail a cab. She hoped this would be an easy task and that she could get to the hospital quickly. *I can do it*, she egged herself on. *I'm strong*.

Wendell's eyes had been closed, just like Benjie's had been that day she'd found him dead. *But Wendell is strong, he wants to live*, she promised herself. She picked up his large backpack from the ground, pulled out his cell phone, and scrolled through his contacts until she found Josh. She stayed there with the phone in her hand, debating whether or not to call him.

Now she was standing in the slow hospital elevator, impatient to get to the third floor. She watched all the people hurrying in and out to see their loved ones. When she arrived she walked breathlessly into his room. Wendell was lying in bed with his eyes closed. Deedee came nearer and took his hand, not knowing if he was asleep or awake. She held onto his hand for a long time.

"I had such a nice time riding that bike," he said quietly, without opening his eyes. The cool touch of her hand was a relief. "I'm sorry I scared you. But the good news is: dying isn't that easy."

"It is at our age," she said with a tired smile and took a seat by his bed, trying to fight off the self-pity that rose inside her. She hated hospitals, though sometimes these little rooms with the bed and the window seemed like a brief escape from the troubles of the outside world. Every so often she got the urge to become a helpless patient and to just stare at the world from beyond the windows of a detached hospital.

"Turns out I only sprained by wrist," he said with a smile. "I need to stay the night for observation, and first thing tomorrow morning we can head out to Rosie's."

"Your wife can sleep here," said the doctor as he walked into the room, pointing to a second, empty bed in the room.

"I'm not his wife," said Deedee, lying down on the narrow bed. She propped her feet up on a pillow and sighed deeply. "If I'd known I would have to sleep in rickety wooden cabins and hospital beds I'm not sure I would have joined you," she tried to joke.

"Mrs. Parker, I'll be right out in the hallway if you need anything," said a nurse who stuck her head in. "Good night," she added, turning out the light.

"Sleeping at a hospital is one thing," Wendell whispered, "but being referred to as Mrs. Parker is just too much to bear. After all, you barely know me," he mumbled. "I'm nothing but your tour guide."

Deedee glanced at him glumly and pulled the blanket all the way up to her chin.

"Good night," Wendell finally said, watching her sinking into sleep. In the darkness of the room she looked like a little girl, her long hair softly framing her face. He listened to the gentle rustle of her breath and looked out the window at the lights of the city outside. "If you really want to know," he said quietly, aware that she was already asleep, "being Mrs. Parker isn't all that bad…"

Early the next morning, before the sun came up,

Deedee woke up and washed her face with lukewarm water at the sink by the bed. Then she brushed her teeth with a plastic wrapped tooth brush she'd found in the room and fixed her hair. In spite of the many years she'd been alive, she could never get used to the heaviness that filled her each morning. She loathed the sensation.

By the time she walked outside the sun was shining brightly in spite of the frosty cold. She sat down on a metal bench in the hallway outside of Wendell's room and looked at the tall snow dripping maple trees outside the window.

Wendell awoke shortly thereafter, got out of bed, and went to wash his face, mumbling an old folk song that was echoing inside his head:

"What shall we do with the drunken sailor?

What shall we do with the drunken sailor?

What shall we do with the drunken sailor?

Early in the morning…"

He sat down on the bed to put on his jacket when he realized how difficult it would be to do this with a cast on his arm. He draped the jacket gently over his shoulders. "Oh, well," he said out loud. He wanted to get out of the hospital. The odor of cleaning substances and the voices of doctors and patients out in the hallway urged him to go on with his interrupted trip. He looked around for his backpack when his eyes fell on a young man standing in the doorway. The man looked at him awkwardly, a small smile twitching in the corners of his mouth.

"Jesus Christ," Wendell cried. He sat back down on the bed, baffled at the sight of the young man. "What are you doing here?"

"Hey, Dad," the man said and walked over hesitantly. He leaned down and wrapped his arms tightly around his father's bony shoulders. Wendell froze at the familiar touch, a touch he'd mostly only imagined. By the time he finally got a hold of himself and wanted to hug back, Josh had already pulled away, folding his arms in his lap, as if his arms were an extension of his heart, keeping it from harm, protecting himself.

"Did Deedee call you?" Wendell asked quietly, fighting a tear that wanted to leave his eye.

"Yes. Yesterday afternoon. She asked that I come. She said you probably broke your leg, falling off a bicycle? I got on the first flight out of California."

"She didn't tell me she called... how pointless of her

to make you worry." Wendell's eyes lingered on Josh and he sighed. "Your old man isn't going anywhere just yet."

They hadn't seen each other in over a year. Josh was relieved to see his father in good shape. When Deedee called he was sure this was goodbye, and his mind was heavy with thoughts the entire flight over.

"Come on, let's get out of here," said Wendell, getting to his feet and allowing Josh to carry his backpack. Though they hadn't seen each other in a long time, and though there were many things they didn't know about each other, they always remembered the feeling of being father and son, painfully dear to one another, a love accompanied by great unrest.

They took the elevator in silence. For a moment, their eyes met, and Wendell noticed a twinkle shining in Josh's eye. For the first time, he noticed that his son projected a pure, beaming, masculine energy.

"I didn't know you were back in New Jersey," Josh finally said, breaking the silence.

***

Deedee met them downstairs at the main hall. "You look so sweet together," she said, smiling. She tried not to meet Wendell's eye. "I thought his leg was broken and that I wouldn't be able to take care of him by myself, and someone had to get the car from the park," she said apologetically to Josh, really aiming her explanations at Wendell.

"Shall we get some breakfast?" Asked Josh. He was hungry after his long flight and wanted to break the awkward atmosphere. He wondered about this odd scenario he'd walked into: his father and this Deedee person, traveling together.

The spacious café was lively. Morning voices emerged from every corner: people chatted, a group of girls giggled ceaselessly, and trays of juice and sandwiches traveled from the kitchen to the tables. The three of them sat at a round corner table and ate silently, bowls of steaming oatmeal with cinnamon. Wendell added more and more handfuls of dark raisins to his bowl, taking in the sugar contained in those dry grapey morsels. "God, I needed this food," he finally said, wiping his mouth with a napkin.

"So what are you two even doing here in the first place?" Josh finally asked.

"Do you mean to say that, legally, at our advanced age we were meant to stay home with a caretaker holding our hands as we walk down the street?"

"Legally, you ought to," Josh said with a smile.

"God help us," said Deedee, looking at them gravely. "I'd never want a stranger living with me and taking care of me. How awful, to have to pay someone to take care of me." Now she focused her gaze on Josh's brown eyes. "We're going to visit my sister," she said. "She's sick." Then she smiled and added, "We were only planning to be away for a few days, but our plans keep getting thwarted, as if we were the protagonists of an adventure movie."

Josh nodded wordlessly. The rumbling silence stretched between the two men like a thread. When she finished eating, Deedee hung her yellow purse over her arm and announced, "I'm going to leave you two alone. You haven't seen each other in a long time. There's a library across the street. I'll go read and relax a little."

Wendell said nothing, only watching her as she got up, leaning against the table, pleading with her legs to cooperate, the way one might try to reason with a stubborn dog. The sidewalks were covered with a thin layer of frost, and tall heaps of snow piled at the curbs. *It's like a snow desert*, Deedee thought as she stepped out into the chilly street and walked slowly among the ice patches, careful not to slip. She knew that one misplaced step could enter her into the sad statistic of old people who break a hip and expedite their shameful ailing helplessness.

With aching feet, tired from the disrupted sleep of a hospital bed, she finally walked into the Portland Public Library and looked around, impressed. The lobby was much larger and more elegant than the one in the small library back home. A row of round windows along the high walls made her feel especially small, almost invisible. She wandered slowly, taking in the expanses, inhaling the familiar aroma of old books standing silently on shelves, inviting her to disappear into other worlds. A colorful sign on the bulletin board caught her eye:

Wild Hearts Can't Be Broken

Love Poetry Reading, Friday, November 16th

Come for an afternoon of joyful and melancholic love poetry. Bring your work and read it in front of a live audience.

She lingered for several minutes in front of the sign, then, without thinking too much, as if her feet had made the decision for her, she followed a group of people who walked into a cozy room off the lobby. *It must be starting now*, she thought with excitement. She hadn't attended a poetry reading in years. Not since before Benjie died.

***

"How are you, Son?" Wendell finally dared ask, trying to burrow through Josh's armor with his eyes.

"I'm fine," said Josh, a little distant. He didn't like how uncomfortable he felt whenever his father looked at him directly. It was painful.

The waitress arrived to clear the empty plates. One by one she placed them in a big plastic bin, wiping the crumbs away with a wet paper towel.

Wendell looked at the empty table and felt a lump of sadness crawling into his throat. "I know we've never talked about it. I… I had to leave back then," he said hesitantly, choosing his words carefully. "I don't think I ever told you why I couldn't stay. I don't think I even knew."

"I don't want to talk about the past," Josh said, cutting him off, trying to retain his businesslike tone.

"Fine. But I want you to know I came back from England after all these years because I wanted to be closer to you and make up for lost time." Wendell's face twisted with pain.

"You came back because you're getting too old to be a wanderer," Josh answered cynically, holding steadfast to his defenses.

"You're so wrong," Wendell murmured, feeling a pinch of insult at the bottom of his chest.

"I don't want to fight with you again," said Josh. "The last few times we met we were both left feeling like little flies that were stomped to death."

Wendell sipped his hot tea. The bits of lemon inside it left a sour taste in his mouth. "How's James?" He finally asked, trying to change the subject. "Is he still a troublemaker?"

"A big troublemaker," said Josh, trying once again to regain his calm. "Yesterday he decided to experiment with watercolors on the living room wall."

"That's good," said Wendell, trying to smile. "Now is the only time he can still get away with that kind of behavior."

Josh said nothing, looking at his father. Their best intentions were evaporating into the air of the café like drops of boiling water spraying from a pot. He took a few sips of water and wondered if it was time to go.

"You see, two hours with you and I feel all of my demons about to break out," he suddenly told his father. "I hoped I'd be able to control it this time, you know? The whole way over here I kept telling myself you're a poor old man, and that I'd best let go of my anger rather than fall into this trap like I always do." He stood up and sat back down, disappointed with himself for failing to keep his cool. His armor was cracking. "And you know what really gets to me?" he asked, looking at Wendell, who was crouching meekly in his seat. "Children can't help but love their parents. It's something we're born with. It's involuntary, a survival instinct. A child will love his parent to the death, even if the parent hurts him." Josh fell silent and sighed deeply. "God damn you," he said and looked out onto the busy street outside. "A child can never... A child is just a child, he doesn't have the power to deal with this kind of thing..." Josh's voice was cracking, on the verge of tears.

Wendell pulled his chair closer to his son's and said softly, "I'm sorry. I don't deserve your forgiveness, but I'm going to ask for it anyway." He rubbed Josh's hand with his wrinkled, emaciated hand, and felt his heart contracting at the sight of tears in his son's eyes.

"I'm very proud of you," he said.

Josh gave him a long look, examining the man's lined face and his skin, which was loose like tarp. *How pointless, to go on being mad at this old man for moments long gone*, he thought. He knew that deep inside, Wendell had always loved him intensely. "I'm going to have to go back soon," said Josh, shaking off the remains of his hurt. "It's a busy day on the farm and people are waiting for me. Are you going to be all right?"

"Of course," said Wendell, taking a long sip of his tea.

Josh stood up, shouldered his backpack, and slipped his cell phone into his pocket. He gave his father a light hug, careful not to touch the cast arm. His body revealed the concern he did not put into words.

"Thanks for coming, Kid," Wendell said, attempting to return to his normal tone. Tears pooled in the corners of his eyes. He watched Josh disappearing down the street, then left the café as well, crossing the busy street toward the library. *Thank God for Deedee*, he thought. In spite of her critical, worried face, he was so glad to have her waiting there for him. Thanks to her, he wasn't all alone in this world.

***

It was already late afternoon when Deedee Field stood in the center of a room, right in the middle of a semi-circle of chairs, wearing a light turtleneck sweater. She held a thick notebook with a faded cover and read a poem she'd written the night before her Birthday, speaking the words slowly and evocatively:

...."*The years go by. My eightieth birthday marks the passing years with heavy, absentminded stomps. Time, which used to spread before me like an enormous carpet of possibilities and endless discoveries, diminishes into a small, dusty carpet covered in uneven footprints, under which the missed opportunities and shards of my life are swept.*

Birthday. A quiet reminder of my arrival in this world, the first day in which I emerged from a warm, safe womb into a cold, naked world. Little children are eager to celebrate their birthday. They look forward to it all year long, talking and thinking about their party, imagining the shape, size, and color of their birthday cake.

Meanwhile, adults celebrate with a kind of matter-of-fact formality. Even the gifts they ask for are transformed from bicycles and magic wands into vacations or a massage. Indeed, as age increases, so does the burden on one's back, requiring constant relief. And maybe the difference is in the fact that children look forward to their birthday as a symbol of their growth, while adults only see it as another milestone in their wilting. ..."

She didn't notice Wendell standing among the audience, listening intently. When she finished reading she cleared the stage for the next reader with flushed cheeks and a demure smile that drew back onto her face when she noticed him. He fixed his big eyes on her. "That was beautiful, Deedee," he said in a terribly serious voice. "Beautiful and real."

When the reading was over they sat on a bench in a side room. "I was listening to everyone reading and thought to myself, why shouldn't I read my poems as well?" she explained. Her voice revealed her excitement.

"I'd like to hear more," he said, glancing at her notebook.

"Maybe later, if I'm still feeling this silly. How did it go with Josh? I'm sorry I didn't tell you I'd called him. I should have told you. I—"

"It's all right," he cut her off. "I understand. You panicked."

She was surprised by how quickly he was willing to let it go.

"We didn't get a chance to talk very much. He had to get going," Wendell said, looking away from her, trying as hard as he could not to show her how sad he truly felt. But Deedee didn't need to see his eyes to know. She could tell by the way he slumped in his seat, and her heart ached for him. "Maybe it's for the best," he continued. "At least we didn't fight. When we said goodbye he looked at me with concerned eyes and I could see myself when I was his age. That was exactly how I used to look at my father's aging face. It hurt to realize I was losing him while he was still there, gradually saying goodbye to him. I know how much I let him down." Wendell lowered his eyes and rubbed a tissue between his fingers as his eyes began to well up. "My father was a difficult man," he said. "He yelled at us all the time. He had daily fits of rage. I remember being a child and hearing him yelling at me from the other room as I played, then running over to my mother for protection. Sometimes I stopped playing before he even began yelling, too anxious to play. When Josh was a baby, I found myself becoming furious at him for no apparent reason. I was impatient and hotheaded. I was appalled to find that my father's demons did not disappear when he died but transferred into me. After a few months of inner turmoil I finally left home. I did it for his sake. I didn't want to hurt him. I didn't want to put him through what I'd been through. You see, he grew up without a father, but he had a normal, quiet childhood. His mother raised him well." He looked at Deedee through pained eyes. "Nobody tells you the only parent you can be, at least to begin with, is an imitation of your own. I needed to live alone for many years to realize that, and by the time I did it was already too late."

Deedee listened carefully, trying to connect the sweet, amiable Wendell she'd known to the demons he was talking about. It was a part of him she'd never encountered.

"Our demons live deep inside of us, but they emerge precisely with the people who love us the most," he said quietly, closing his eyes. He was sad but relieved to have shared this burden with someone.

"Oh, Wendell, I… I don't know what to say. That's so sad. I've always wondered why you'd left. We've never talked about it. You didn't tell, and I didn't ask."

They continued to sit on the bench. From time to time people passed them by, searching for a book. Deedee's legs were crossed, her notebook resting on her lap. Wendell glanced out the large windows. The last rays of sun were fading. The cloudy skies made the street lights fade.

"When I was four or five years old, I don't remember exactly, my father took me to a swimming pool. Before I even knew what was happening, he pushed me in. *Time to learn how to swim, Wendell. Go on, swim*, I heard him shouting at me. I tried to keep my head above water, fighting gravity, flailing. But my body kept becoming submerged and my mouth was filled with water. I must have passed out, because the next thing I remember is throwing up and the burning smell of chlorine. That's why I learned how to hold my breath for so long. It was my little way of protecting myself."

"Dear God, Wendell, I had no idea." She closed her

eyes, trying to process this new information. She placed her palm on his cold hand.

Wendell's eyes were still wet, but he didn't cry, not because he didn't want to, but because the tears simply wouldn't come.

"From what you've told me, it sounds like Josh is a compensation for you and your father. You make him sound like such a kind, gentle father. He broke the vicious cycle. If you had stayed, that might have never happened."

"Maybe," he said meekly. "I become helpless when I think about how much pain our parents caused us. Without meaning to, we inherited their sicknesses."

She was surprised by her friend's sudden frankness. She sighed deeply. "Rosie once told me that we're like arrows that had been shot but never reached their aim. This was at the point when everyone she knew was married and having children, and only she remained single. Her arrow hit too many obstacles along its path. Sometimes our arrow goes through so much that it misses its initial aim."

"My father never apologized, but I forgave him. I learned to love him after he died. Only after I did that was I able to forgive myself for not being the kind of father Josh deserved."

They left the library and walked slowly down the street. The chill of winter invaded their jackets, piercing their skin. Deedee came closer and said, "I truly did want to die before I came on this trip with you."

"I know."

"And now my heart is glad that I'm still here."

Wendell said nothing, only squeezing her hand. A cloud of melancholy enveloped them, alongside a certain sweetness they found in their intimacy. If it weren't so cold they would have probably walked some more. It was a full moon, the sky glowing white.

They crossed the street and entered a little old pub with wood paneled walls and pictures of legendary football players. An old man wearing a newsboy cap stood in the corner, playing a wailing fiddle. They sat down at a corner table, letting their eyes adjust to the dim lighting.

"I like the fiddle. It's a little happy and a little sad," said Wendell. "Just like life."

"That's the same reason I like grapefruits—they're a little bitter and a little sweet. As you get older, you get used to the bitterness that follows the initial sweetness."

The fiddle player began to play an Irish folk tune, the sounds filling the pub with cheer.

"Will you dance with me?" Wendell suddenly asked, rising slowly from his seat. "Even though your legs hurt and my arm hurts?" He smiled bashfully.

Deedee's eyes were wide and glittery, like a little girl's. She stood up and wrapped her arms around his shoulders, hesitantly at first, then tightening her grip. The two of them moved to the sounds of the fiddle.

"I like to dance," he whispered into her ear. "I haven't done it in so long… this is when my soul roams free."

They swayed slowly in each other's arms. She could smell Wendell's shaving cream and the cookies he'd eaten earlier. She rested her head on his shoulder and closed her eyes.

***

Wendell leaned against the pillow. He'd had too much to drink the night before. Something like three glasses of wine, after not drinking for so long. His head felt heavy, beaten by persistent little hammers. He glanced at

Deedee on the bed next to him. She was still sleeping at 11 a.m. *Well, well,* he thought. *Two glasses of wine and the industrious early-riser becomes a hibernator.*

They'd stayed in the pub until the small hours of the night, a time in which she'd normally only be awake if she'd already woken up for the day, back in her home life which now seemed so far away. With the last of their strength they were able to falter into a small motel across the street. The yawning receptionist wasn't sure if he was dreaming or if too old drunks really did stumble into the hotel at four in the morning, asking for a room with two single beds. He informed them that he only had a room with one double bed, and they had no choice but to agree. Wendell had too pee very badly and was so tired he could barely speak.

Deedee stirred and opened her eyes. At first she smiled, but when she realized that Wendell was in bed with her, under the covers, she jumped up and sat on the edge of the bed.

"Good morning," he said. "Well, it's almost noon, actually, but that's the whole point of a vacation."

She looked at him, befuddled.

"Last night was amazing," he said. "One of the

best I've ever had."

"Last night...?" She mumbled.

"I don't remember all of it, only that we got here and you took off your clothes and walked over to me."

She looked down at her body with alarm, then saw that she was still wearing yesterday's clothes. She flushed with embarrassment.

"I'm just kidding," he said. "The truth is I was barely able to drag you in here, and when we got to the room you collapsed like a tree and slept until just now."

Deedee grabbed her head and twisted her face.

"I know," he said, "my head hurts too. I can barely keep my eyes open."

"God, Wendell, how stupid can we be? At our age that much alcohol could kill us."

"Maybe," he said, amused, "but on the other hand, it might have brought us back to life."

Deedee got up and went to the bathroom, surprised by how quickly her feet had obeyed her. She turned on the water in the faucet and then looked at her reflection. Her face was so puffy with sleep that she had trouble opening her eyes all the way. The fact that she couldn't remember anything of the previous night embarrassed her. Then she went to her pink toiletry kit, pulled out some pain medication, took two pills and offered one to Wendell, along with a tall glass of water.

"This might sound odd," he said after taking the pill, "but I'm happy to have this headache. It reminds me of being young, drinking a lot, enjoying life. Those were the good old days. I guess sometimes you need to feel pain to know you're alive."

Deedee looked at the pill bottles in her bag, wondering if she'd manage to take all her various daily medications while feeling like she'd been run over. Outside the window, a gray little squirrel scurried around, hopping lightly over the snow. She watched, mesmerized by its agility as it hopped from one tree to the next without falling. "If I had to choose one animal I identify with," she said, "it would be a squirrel. It's scared of every little thing, but performs the bravest acts." She took another sip of her water.

"Squirrels also bite," Wendell offered. "Just like that, without giving any warning."

"They do?" she marveled. "How can they bite if they never approach people?"

"Sometimes they do approach people."

"How about you? What animal do you identify with?"

Wendell paused. "That's a great question. Let me think about it."

"No, please, don't think. Say the first thing that comes to mind."

"I don't know... maybe a wild horse? No, you know what just came to mind?"

"What?"

"A cow."

"A cow?!"

"Yes. Cows always look so peaceful, almost indifferent. The troubles of the world are never apparent on their faces."

Deedee was disappointed. "I was sure you were going to say a dog. They have a joyfulness that reminds me of you."

"I love dogs, for sure. But they tend to be demure and take the fault for crimes they didn't commit. And I think a gazelle is more suitable for you than a squirrel."

"A gazelle?" she wondered. "But it's so vulnerable and always being hunted. I hope I'm stronger than that," she said, smiling.

Wendell lay back down. "You know, my father was a hunter. One time, when I was about eleven years old, he brought home a rabbit, brought it straight into the kitchen. It was still dripping blood, and its head was hanging, lifeless, from its little body. He skinned it and dissected it on a cutting board as if he were cutting vegetables for a salad. The sink filled up to the rim with bright red blood. When he was finished, he offered me the tail as a toy. I went to my bedroom and stood there, shocked, holding the tail in my hand. It felt velvety, almost addictive. I kept running my hand over it. It was a gift from my father and I wanted to enjoy it, but I couldn't. I was too sad about the rabbit. I remember I played with the tail for a few days as it spread a weird aroma in my room, kind of reminiscent of new shoes. At dinner, my parents ate the rabbit, roasted in onions and garlic. I had a little bite. It was so dry that I almost threw up. It's odd how memories come up uninvited. I can't remember the house I lived in five years ago or the people I used to be friends with before I came back to New Jersey, but I remember the color of that tail from over seventy years ago.

I remember a conversation we had a few months

before he died. I asked him how he was, and he said he was tired, having hunted all night. *The best time to go is before dawn,* he said, *when the animals come out of hiding, feeling safe to roam.* He sat on a small ladder in the dark woods, holding a flashlight and waiting for hours for the deer to come. Finally, at four in the morning, a gazelle and a fawn appeared. Surprised by the flashlight, they froze, staring at him. After he told me this there was a long silence. Eventually I asked: *Did you shoot them? No,* he said quietly. *Why not?* I was confused. *I felt sorry for them,* he said in a voice that sounded sad, though to this day I'm not sure about that. He might have just been tired or apathetic. He died a few months later."

Deedee lay down beside him, listening to the birds chirping outside. It began to snow, and she wondered how birds could live in such cold weather. The cold made her think their chirping was weaker than regular birdsong. Wendell placed a moist towel on his face to ease his headache. "I haven't thought about him in years. I don't know where all these memories are coming from. I guess meeting Josh took me back to a different time."

"Maybe the older we get the more childish we

become," she said, looking outside, searching for the birds she'd heard. "And also," she began, then paused, breathed, and continued, "maybe we'll meet our parents in heaven soon. They say when you die you see your family."

"I don't believe that," he said gruffly. "It's too naïve. At any rate, I hope it isn't true. I really don't want to meet my old man up there."

Deedee laughed. "Well, she said, if it is true, he'd be different when you meet him. It would be only his soul. The rough man would be gone. Rosie always used to believe that. She thought when she left this world she'd meet our mother again. When I die I want my ashes scattered in a flower field. That way, a part of me will always remain in the endless expanses of this world. I don't want a coffin burial."

"Well, then you'd better die in the summer," he said, a smile pinching the corners of his mouth. "As you know, flowers don't bloom in winter…" Then he turned serious. "I don't really think anyone can choose their death," he said. "Only their life, and that's what counts." He sighed deeply and put his head in his hands. "We'll stay here today and rest. I can't go anywhere with this headache. Maybe some wine would help?" he joked, covering himself with the blanket. "I'm so tired. All I can think about is eating mashed potatoes that melt in your mouth and chocolate cake with thick icing that cracks between your teeth."

Deedee smiled. "Not a bad idea," she said.

"Really?" He turned to her, surprised. "I was sure you were going to say you needed green juice."

"I do need green juice. But I'd also have a slice of cake."

Wendell's toes peeked out from under the blanket. While he was tall, Deedee was shorter than average. She watched as his long body curled up to fit the mattress. His head was still adorned with a yellow tuft of hair, and white hair showed on his chest from the opening of his shirt. *Oh God*, she thought. *How will we sleep here in the same bed?*

As if reading her mind, he mumbled sleepily, "I'm wearing pajamas, don't worry." Then he sank into a deep sleep, his snores filling the room.

She lay on the edge of the bed, careful not to touch his body, which was rising and falling rhythmically. She lay beside him for a long time, fully awake,

pondering the words he'd written to her in his note
before they embarked on this trip: "People don't die of
old age, they die of loneliness."

Wendell lay on his back, his cast arm resting on
his belly, a serene look on his face. His presence made
her feel warm and safe. In the quiet she'd forgotten
existed, away from the drumrolls of the great big world,
this tall, old man appeared to remind her just how
beautiful she really was.

***

They only had four hours to go until they reached
Rosie's house. Deedee still felt a little nauseated from
their night of drinking, but also from her anticipation of
her meeting with her sister. She looked out the window
at the fields that grayed with cold.

"What are you thinking about?" he asked.

"Last night, before I went to bed, I thought about
how old age is like a caterpillar. Old people are
convinced they're going to die, but we don't know
what's going to happen, just like the caterpillar doesn't
know it will become a butterfly. Maybe something good
will happen to us after we die, Wendell?"

"I don't think anyone can tell what happens after

you die, Deedee, but I can promise you that something good can happen to us while we're alive."

They reached Sullivan in the late afternoon. A bone-chilling cold greeted them as they drove into town. They passed an old church at the entrance to Rosie's small street. A line of people were making their way out of the Sunday morning mass, coming down the stone steps. Wendell hadn't been to a church since he was nine years old. He looked at the people thoughtfully. "If there's only one God, how could there be so many religions? I'm not sure even the big man upstairs can answer that one…"

"I suppose there are many ways of reaching Him," Deedee said with a restless smile. Her eyes were focused on Rosie's house, which she could already see at the edge of the street. They continued to drive along the street until it turned into a dirt path flanked by thorny bushes. When the path came to an end Wendell turned off the engine. Deedee stepped slowly into the cold sun, stretching her arms, which had stiffened during the ride. A flock of white butterflies flew before her, gently fluttering their thin wings. With small, measured steps, she walked to the front door, lingering there. Finally, she knocked twice, then listened to hesitant steps approaching but waited for a long time before the door opened. In the doorway was a heavy-set moonfaced young woman wearing large glasses. Deedee didn't recognize her. The woman stared at her for a moment, then said, "Are you Deedee?"

Deedee nodded.

"Your sister died on Friday night. I'm her caretaker. I tried to call you. I'm sorry."

Deedee felt her thoughts racing like galloping horses. The truth is, she had nothing to say. She looked back at Wendell, then stepped inside and sat down on the old brown sofa in the living room. It was just like back then, that moment when she'd seen Benjie lifeless and leaned in to look at his face, feeling the same defeat and the same helplessness. Once again, she found herself faced with the great, endless death, the one that beat us all eventually.

Rosie collected owls. Some of them she bought at yard sales, others she'd ordered online. She had almost forty owls in a variety of colors and sizes, some ceramic, others glass, others yet crocheted, adorned with a delicate handmade pattern. On her rare visits, Deedee always thought the owls were looking at her funny. Now she glanced morbidly at the dusty owls on the shelf. Across from the door was Rosie's old piano, wrinkled sheet music lying on its ledge. She walked over and sat on the small wooden piano bench, taking a deep breath. For a moment, she thought she smelled Rosie's familiar scent, a mixture of lavender soap and apple pie. She remained sitting for a long moment, knowing that when she stood up, Rosie's strong presence would evaporate.

On the piano was a small vase with a wilted rose. She took hold of the rose and rubbed its leaves between her fingers. Suddenly, Wendell appeared by her side, gently putting his arms around her shoulders. "I'm sorry," he said quietly. She closed her eyes and buried her head in his lap.

"One day, when we're older, Mama and Papa will die," Rosie once told her when they were little.

"I can't even think about that. It'll never happen," she had answered.

"Sadly, it will, Deedee. But we'll be together, and we'll hold each other tight…"

She sipped some of the water that Rosie's caretaker had brought her. It was bitter and she could barely get it down.

"She died two nights ago in her sleep."
When I got here at eight o'clock yesterday morning I
found her in bed. Her face was more peaceful than I'd
ever seen it. She called a few days ago to wish you a
happy birthday, but there was no answer."

Deedee looked at her. Tears began streaming down
her face.

"I hope you can find comfort in knowing she's free
now, free of her pain," the woman said and patted
Deedee's shoulder. "She was very sick toward the end. I
came in this morning to give the place a last cleaning.
I'm so sorry."

Deedee stared at the dull walls. Who loved her in
her final months? Who made her smile at night before
she fell asleep? Other than Alma, Deedee's daughter, a
handful of acquaintances at their hometown, there was
nobody to inform. She left this life just as she'd lived it:
in utter solitude. Deedee went into the bathroom, looked
at Rosie's white bathrobe hanging from a hook on the
wall, and washed her face with cold water, fighting off
her tears. Snowflakes were coming down outside,
carpeting the garden elegant white.

And Rosie was gone… her soul roaming free in invisible worlds, just at the moment when Deedee wanted so badly to embrace her, to share memories of their childhood, when they were little and waiting for big things to happen, to feel her presence one last time, to say goodbye. Death, she thought, was always more painful for those who stayed behind.

"We need to pack up these silly owls and donate them to charity," she told Wendell when she finally came out of the bathroom. She saw no point in keeping items for their sentimental value, nor did she feel compelled to cry over cookbooks and the old mementos of the dead. All she truly wanted to do at that moment was return to her home in the sleepy suburb, put on warm slippers and make her green juice and beloved oatmeal with some cinnamon and maple syrup.

She called Alma, to give her the news. The two of them hadn't spoken since Deedee had left on this trip with Wendell. Now she did her best to sound strong and retain a steady voice, though inside she was in agony. Soon, Rosie would be buried in the ground, and there would be no one in the world to remember her but the two of them.

Deedee put on her coat. "I think I'll take a little walk," she said.

"Want me to go with you?" Wendell asked. Without waiting for a response, he put on his boots and followed her outside. The two of them walked slowly down the path, following the footprints left on the soft snow. A few days ago her sister still took her morning walk down this street, and now she was gone. Mere seconds separated here from there, like the fragile space between two heartbeats. One moment you're here, the next you're gone. A gust of cold air energized her. She took a few deep breaths. "Now that Mama and Rosie are gone, I guess I'm next," she said.

"Or maybe I am," Wendell said with a sad smile and picked up a small acorn.

"Want to bet?"

"I would, but if I win I won't be around to see you lose. Anyway, Deedee, we're still here, free."

"Free? I'm not so sure about that."

"Well, I'm free," he said, then said, "well, sometimes." He threw the acorn back onto the ground and watched it rolling slowly and coming to a stop in the middle of the road.

Deedee looked at him. His thoughtful gaze and the cookie crumbs on his shirt collar made her smile for the first time since they'd arrived.

He looked back at her. Her agonized face made him want to give her a warm, long hug, but instead he looked away toward the trees on the side of the road without saying a word.

They walked past the church, which was now empty and turning white with snow.

"Wendell," Deedee said quietly. "Have you ever wondered what happens the moment after you die?"

"I don't know," he said calmly. "Maybe it feels like before being born?"

It was getting dark. A cold wind beat against the branches. The two of them returned to Rosie's home and made beds on the living room sofas. The funeral would take place the next morning. How dark and orphaned this house, which once contained a life and now didn't, looked to her. She wondered if there was a place in the sky where souls returns once their bodies died.

The next day, in the early afternoon, right after the funeral, Wendell waited for her in the warm car. Deedee took a seat beside him wordlessly. Neither of them could stay at Rosie's house a moment longer. A cloud of discontent familiar to anyone who's ever attended a funeral filled the car. These were moments of no comfort. All Deedee wanted was for time to pass and her thoughts to return to daily troubles, ones that didn't hurt too much. Her legs felt terribly weak. She'd been suffering from arthritis for some years now, and there was no joint in her body that didn't ache.

In spite of the heat inside the car, Wendell still felt cold. He tried to say something, but the words refused to come out. "I think we should start heading back home," he finally managed. "We're eleven hours away from New Jersey. We'll have a nice ride home." The word "home" sounded foreign, coming from him. For the past thirty years he's changed dwellings so many times, far away from his origins. Through the years, the concept of home had become in his mind a temporary place to lay his head at the end of the day. During long, lonely weekends, he liked to listen to music and watch passersby through the window. For people like him, born wanderers, home was where their heart was. This was more than just a cliché to him. For years, he'd taught himself to live in places he was curious about, places that allowed him to reunite with his heart. And when he lost interest in a place, he moved on to someplace new. He was licensed as an English teacher and was lucky enough to always find unusual schools that were willing to accept him for a limited time. Since he lived alone for most of his life, he was able to save enough money for his retirement, which had arrived before he knew it.

"Do you mean your home in New Jersey?" Deedee asked with surprise.

"Yes. Even wild horses like me want to go home sometime."

"I guess you're finally growing up," she smiled. The thought of going home made her feel relief, but another part of her wasn't so sure she wanted to go home yet, and preferred to keep going.

They drove for a long time before Wendell stopped in one of the godforsaken New York State towns along the highway. Hungry and stiff, they walked up a path, Wendell leading with his large strides, Deedee limping behind him with small steps. At the edge of the path, Wendell spotted a small farm with a large wooden home at its center, its white paint chipping. An old red picket fence surrounded the yard. Out front, a "For Sale" sign was pinned into the ground. He came closer and took down the phone number and the name of the real estate agent. "Perhaps I'll buy this house," he said, taking a seat on a small wooden bench outside, looking around curiously. "I have some savings, and I've been toying with the idea of finding a little place out in the country, where I can do all the creative things I've been dreaming of for years." This place was filling his heart with joy.

"Won't you be lonely out here, all alone with these fields and trees?" she asked. She sat beside him on the bench and looked around restlessly. The house, perched alone in nature, made her uncomfortable.

"Being in nature sooths me," he said simply and looked at her, trying to interpret her expression. "Besides, I won't be lonely if you come with me."

She said nothing, stunned by this intimate invitation.

He looked at her again, appearing to rethink his offer. "One of the best things old age has taught me is not to worry so much about what other people think of me. I'd be happy if you lived by my side. That's what I meant to say. And I don't plan on feeling embarrassed about it, even if you say no." With that, Wendell stood up and walked toward the yard.

She watched him walking away, flushed, forgetting all about her hunger. Her hair was wild.

"Deedee?"

"Yes?"

"Did you ever love me?"

"Yes, of course. I've... always loved you."

"But how? The way you love an adorable puppy?"

"No!"

"Then how?"

"The way you love an old friend..."

"Deedee..."

"Yes?"

"Romantic love. Could you ever think of me in those terms?"

"Oh, well, that's... Wendell... I truly don't know."

She was a different person back then. Her thoughts and ponderings had long since scattered like the pollen of old dandelions. His serious, alert face made her smile, and the ice was broken once again. "Romantic love is for the young," she finally said, though she wasn't sure she believed that.

"That isn't fair," Wendell protested, determined not

to give up until she admitted what was in her heart. "Old folks like us are also entitled to feelings."

They walked toward the fields surrounding the house. He was liking this place more and more, listening longingly to the wind blowing through the tops of the trees. A part of him truly did want to stay there in spite of the cold of winter, in spite of the loneliness.

This was the essence of his existence as a natural wanderer. While others sought the safe skyscrapers of busy cities in order to feel safety and comfort at the end of their life, he yearned for nature, for mother earth, for a place where he could watch the seasons change and feel clumps of dirt warmly tickling his feet on warm days. He saw old age as his final days of freedom, an opportunity to make his last dreams come true.

"I think so," she suddenly said when they were back in the Mustang. The car was now speckled with mud, and the two of them were exhausted from the long walk and flushed from cold. Wendell pulled out pine needles that had clung to his sleeve and tossed them out the window. He wasn't following. "Remind me," he said, "what were we talking about?"

"Yes… I once loved you, Wendell," she said,

embarrassed, lowering her eyes and crushing the wool of her cap between her fingers. "Back before you moved to England. I was... in love with you. For a whole year after you left I still hoped you'd come back. Every letter I got from you made me hopeful as if we were an actual couple. I'd read it and reread it, searching it for signs of similar emotions on your end. You always addressed me as "Dear Dee" and I wondered if that was a sign of your affection. I remember one letter where you described the marathon you'd been in, where you came in third. You wrote about your daily runs, how they always starts out hard and then the body grows used to the motion and begins to enjoy it. *The body*, you wrote, *surpasses pain and begins to float.*"

Wendell was taken aback. He looked like a man who'd gotten off the train at the wrong station and was trying to figure out where he was. He removed his hat and scratched his head, back and forth. Then he looked at her with sad eyes. "You... you remember my letters?" he asked, astonished. "I... I don't know what to say, Deedee. I didn't think you ever thought of me that way... I had no idea... you never gave me any indication."

"Of course not," she said with a smile. "Young women don't admit things like that to the men they like." She couldn't help but wonder if her sudden sincerity would change her in his eyes. "It ended when I received your last letter, where you wrote about Suzy, Josh's mother. That's when I realized I should move on. I was twenty-one years old and had all sorts of unrealistic ideas, and that must have been one of them." It felt embarrassing to share this information sixty years after the fact, as if it might demean her in his eyes. On the other hand, she was glad to finally reveal what had been burdening her for all these years. Now, after so much time, it didn't sound so dramatic to her anymore. Just another piquant detail of their past.

Wendell looked at her pale face, the wrinkles that seemed to be chiseled by an artist. The blue of her eyes made them look infinitely deep, and he liked to dive into them. The truth was, he barely remembered their friendship before he'd left. It was as if a locked iron gate was separating him from that time. "Why didn't you tell me?" he asked.

"I didn't think you'd want me. I wasn't the kind of woman you were attracted to."

"The kind of woman I'm attracted to? I don't think that definition exists, Deedee."

"Maybe it used to… I felt that you loved me like a sister, that I was too primpy for you, with my pressed clothes and my combed hair. You wanted a woman to travel with you in nature, wearing boots, not washing her hair for a week, because freedom was more important than anything else." She smiled sadly. "No one knew that I loved you. Just like the poems I wrote all these years, I didn't think anyone would care."

Wendell looked out onto the farm's yard. The branches bent and swayed quickly with the strong wind, rubbing against each other. He felt a tug at his heartstrings. She used to be one of his best friends back then. He loved her inner world, which was as wide as the ocean, and appreciated the fact that she was so self-sufficient, unlike most people, who always needed someone around them. He was the same way. The fact that she had wanted him as a partner made him both embarrassed and proud. He didn't know what to say, and so he stepped out of the car and shut the door behind him, taking a few steps and pausing in the field. "Deedee… I'm sorry you felt that way."

"People fall in love all the time when they're young, Wendell," she said through the window. She was still holding onto her woolen cap. "Most of them experience lots of disappointment before they find someone who loves them back. That's why I'm glad that romantic love is no longer an issue at our age. Romance leads to heartbreak." When she saw him biting his lips, she looked away and shrunk into her seat.

"Let's go," he said, getting back into the car and starting the engine. "We'd better get some food, we're exhausted." He wanted to tell her that one of the best things that ever happened to her was that he didn't fall in love with her; that he could not have been a supportive partner to her back then. But instead he said nothing. He preferred to keep going. He knew that fixating on the past would help neither of them.

***

It was late at night when they said goodbye outside of Deedee's home.

Wendell placed her silver suitcase inside. "You deserved someone much better than the man I was back then."

In response, she offered a sad smile, feeling relieved

to be in the familiar home that had been waiting for her like an old, loyal dog. She was overcome with tiredness. "Thank you for the trip," she finally said.

Wendell walked back to the car, cringing at the cold air.

Deedee closed the door behind her and hurried to the bedroom, where she pulled clean pajamas out of the closet. Then she brushed her teeth and quickly climbed into her beloved, waiting bed.

Outside, the world bowed down modestly, folding into the dark of night like a tired child parting from a busy day. Wendell returned alone to his small home, only a few minutes' drive away, a home he'd barely lived in for most of his life. He lay down on the sofa and covered himself with a brown woolen blanket, falling asleep in his dirty clothes. He was free, like he'd always wanted to be. But what was this freedom worth if he was alone?

SPRING

March came. In spite of the cold outside, those sensitive enough could feel spring slowly awakening deep in the ground. Like a little growl sprouting into the frozen world outside to announce the imminent return of the sun. Even the birdsong sounded more chipper that morning, as Deedee walked out of her home for her walk, her feet clad in snow boots.

She looked at the strong rays shining from the bright sky, and wondered how she could feel such sorrow when spring was almost there. A small, skinny rabbit snuck into one of the yards and sniffed the icy ground suspiciously. *These rabbits always know when to come out of their warrens*, she thought.

On her way back up the street to her house she spotted him from a distance. At first she was convinced she was imagining things. The sun was in her eyes, preventing her from seeing clearly. She kept going, and by the time she arrived there was no doubt about it: Wendell was standing outside her door. She took a careful look at him. He was wearing a faded black t-shirt, a gray hoody, and a pair of old, washed out jeans with a large tear at the knee. He'd been waiting there for a while, knocking at her door, and was about to turn around and return to his car when he saw her coming toward him.

"What are you doing here?" she asked, making no effort to conceal her excitement.

"I missed you, so I came for a visit," he said frankly.

A silly smile stretched across her face. His surprise visit was the last thing she'd expected that morning. They hadn't seen each other in a few months, ever since he moved into that little farm house in the middle of nowhere. She sighed as she looked him over. "What happened to your pants?"

He looked down at the hole. "Uhm," he cleared his throat. "It's just a little souvenir from my morning walk. I tried to climb over the fence and my jeans got caught. I hadn't noticed until you said something. I drove straight to see you, five hours without stopping." He smiled and looked at her face and hair, wondering if she was glad he came.

Ever since he'd left, Deedee often missed him,

especially the small things he'd introduced into her life. They walked inside and sat down at the kitchen table, and then Deedee went into the kitchen and returned with a slice of fresh, fragrant apple pie she'd baked that morning. She liked to bake on Thursdays and had a regular routine: she cubed the apples, sprinkled them with cinnamon, and cooked them in a thick maple and butter concoction.

Wendell stared at the white plate and the pie. He was famished after his drive and the aroma of the cake fogged his senses, but he pushed the plate aside, brought his chair closer to hers, and looked into her eyes silently.

"Is everything all right? Are you not feeling well?" she asked.

"I don't want to eat pie. I…" his voice broke. "I want a hug." He leaned toward her and craned his neck. "All I want is a hug."

Embarrassed, she wrapped her arms around his neck, and he buried his head in her chest like a toddler seeking comfort in his mother's embrace.

"I don't want to find comfort in food anymore. The sugar in relationships lasts a lot longer," he said, a tear running down his cheek. "This morning on my walk I looked around me and thought how perfect everything was in my little piece of heaven, with the pond and the lone duck floating around, with the wooden beams in the shed. I realized I did everything I loved, but I felt alone. I don't want to be alone anymore," he said, a deep sorrow in his eyes. "I know you think I'm just a geezer."

"You're not a geezer…"

"Sometimes I am. I look just like my grandfather used to look, and I smell just like he used to smell. And I wear my pants way above the belt line, just like he did." Wendell's burning eyes gleamed green as he spoke. The short beard he'd grown made him look like one of the knights of yore, tired and wounded but invincible.

She released herself from the hug and poured some tea for him into a small china cup. "Maybe you've just spent too much time alone with the trees."

Wendell took a long sip. "People get lonely in the city, too," he said, "inside those over-crowded buildings. People go mad with loneliness. Take a walk down the streets of New York City, look into people's faces, and you'll see what I mean."

"Yes, that's true," she said. "I feel lonely too, but I'm lonely by choice." She looked at his fallen face and his wrinkled clothes and felt a maternal urge to protect him.

"That's what I used to think too, Deedee—that I was alone by choice. But now I'm not so sure anymore."

He finished his tea and refused her offer of a refill and of staying the night. He wanted to stay, but was worried he may become too attached to her. As he walked outside she waved to him through the window with a sad smile. Then she cleared the plate and rinsed the two tea cups and left them out to dry, orphaned on the counter.

Was she truly alone by choice? She wondered that night as she crawled into bed. *Strange*, she thought. *I've never asked myself that question before.*

***

And then, one morning in early April, as the sky rose foggy and the toads croaked in the pond outside his house, she appeared. That day back in March, as she lay in bed, she realized that her loneliness was only partially a choice, but mostly a coercion. This realization was too painful for her to go on living her life as she had. She took a train from New York to the nearby town, and from there a taxi to Wendell's new home in the middle of nowhere. The train ride took three hours and fifteen minutes and the taxi was another thirty-five minutes, she told him as he walked over to hug her.

"I have to use the bathroom," she said. "I brought you some apple pie," she called as she disappeared into the house.

He barely heard her. His hearing had faded even more in the past months, but he wasn't too worried about it. His heart fluttered with pure, peaceful joy to finally have her there.

Deedee walked into the living room and wondered about the location of the bathroom. She walked through the bedroom and the laundry room and finally found it.

He was looking forward to her arrival since she'd called earlier that week to tell him she's given the matter a lot of thought, and that maybe the two of them ought to spend some time together. She didn't say "move in together" but only "spend time", and he quite liked the vagueness. The pond, which had been frozen for the past few months, was beginning to thaw, like a bear slowly waking up from hibernation. The days were getting longer, allowing for a beautiful hour of dusk, illuminated by a sweet light. That was her favorite time of day. After recovering from the long ride, she walked back outside and sat down on the bench. The small flowers that Wendell had planted were blooming in purple and yellow. She marveled at them, feeling her heart opening up along with them. Wendell pulled out some weeds from the flowerbed and then took a seat next to her.

"You know when the best time to plant a tree is?" he asked.

"I'm not sure. Spring?"

"No. The best time to plant a tree is twenty years ago. And the second best time is right now. I knew you'd be coming today. I was excited and had trouble falling asleep last night. I have a book of proverbs on my bedside table, so I picked it up last night, and that's the one I read. I usually fall asleep with the TV on, watching a sports game. But I thought in honor of your arrival it would be better to fall asleep with some wisdom on my mind…"

"It's a very nice proverb, Wendell," she said, smiling.

***

Since she'd come the days had been blending into each other, time losing its meaning. Wendell couldn't remember how long it had been since her arrival. Had it been a month or a full season? He woke up every morning around ten, made himself a thick blueberry jam sandwich, and read the morning paper. Sometimes he laughed too loudly, hurting her sensitive ears, and then she would retire to her small room with the yellow curtains and play some sonatas on the stereo. In the afternoon he liked to work in his woodshop and sing at the top of his lungs while he ran the electric saw. She would watch him through the window, smiling forgivingly.

They slept in separate bedrooms, though he would have gladly shared his bed with her. But after the many years she'd spent alone, it was too late to change such deeply ingrained habits. Sometimes, in the evening, as it grew dark, he snuck into her room and sat beside her on her wide bed. She would read to him from whatever book she was reading at the time, until his eyes closed and his head plopped on the pillow beside her, like a small dog, falling asleep unintentionally in a warm corner of a room. Once, she fell asleep too, then woke up in the middle of the night to the sound of his loud snoring. She remained lying next to him, awake, listening to his deep breaths and the sounds of the nocturnal birds outside. Sometimes, when she couldn't sleep, she was visited by an old memory of Benjie, recalling his brown eyes that used to look at her with warmth and worry.

One night, Wendell woke up to the sound of her screaming. He rushed into her bedroom. She was sitting up in bed, her forehead and hair drenched with sweat. "I had a bad dream," she said, startled. Her eyes were wide and terrified. He sat down beside her and offered her the glass of water from her bedside table. "I dreamt I was walking through a thick forest, fighting thorny bushes to get to the other end. Then I woke up," she said, tears streaming down her face. "My tribe. My family. I have no one, Wendell, other than my daughter. Everyone I've ever had is gone. What's the point?"

Wendell watched the moonlight filtering in through the window. "I know those moments of loneliness well," he said, his eyes glowing in the dark room. He came closer, wiping her tears away with his fingers, and said, "Go to sleep, Deedee. It was just a dream."

The next morning he woke up later than usual. He stood in the bathroom and urinated while staring outside the large window, as always, when suddenly he noticed that his Mustang was gone and that the red gate was wide open. He zipped up his pants and hurried outside, barefoot and confused. Then he walked back inside and glanced in the direction of Deedee's bedroom. Was she still asleep? He didn't want to disturb her after the difficult night she'd had. But her bedroom door was ajar, and he could see that her bed was empty, the blue quilt carefully spread over it, the two white ruffled pillows set perfectly atop it.

He went to the closed bathroom door, pressed his ear against it and said, "Deedee? Good morning..." He waited for an answer for what felt like an eternity, then opened the door. The bathroom was empty, as was the toothbrush cup. Only her enormous, floral shower cap was still there. "Oh, Deedee, you can't be serious," he mumbled and went back into her bedroom, plopping down on the bed. He stared at the brown wooden dresser and the vase of purple flowers she'd picked the previous day during her morning walk.

Then he went to the kitchen to make himself some coffee, telling himself she must have run out to buy some celery and leafy greens and would be back in no time. He didn't remember her saying she had to go anywhere, and he knew she hadn't driven a car in over a decade, ever since she sold her own, having decided she shouldn't drive anymore.

He tried to call her cell phone and left a voicemail. "Deedee, Deedee, it's me, Wendell. Umm… if you hear this message, call me back. Bye. Have a nice day. It's me, Wendell."

On a sunny day after the rains stopped I went off to search for myself… what did I expect to find? Long lost childhood memories? Perhaps I only wanted to save myself from myself.

It's been a long time since I've last seen me, and I could no longer remember who I was.

In the mirrors hanging on the wall I kept seeing someone different. Among the illusions of time, all the images were me, and I was them

Every image was of someone I wanted to be and could have been, but I ended up not being any of them.

It happens that once in this long life, the right person appears and helps us meet ourselves again, if only for a few moments. It happens quietly, without any fanfare. Just as we're about to forget, they arrive to remind us how beautiful and special we really are.

For Deedee, that someone was Wendell Parker. Though they hadn't seen each other for years, they maintained a connection that went beyond any geographic distance. Wendell reminded her that keeping the faith was better than losing hope; that holding onto dreams was better than forgetting them; that late was better than never. He was also the one to remind her that, though it was never too late, it could still be much later than we think. In those moments when they lived side by side, she realized how paradoxical people are: when it's time to leave they want to stay, and when it's time to drop anchor and rest, they get the urge to take off.

***

In the evening, after seven o'clock, Wendell became even more worried. He took a seat on the living room chair and uncapped his third beer of the day. His feet were resting on the small living room table, and he was donning Deedee's shower cap in an attempt to cheer himself up. He wasn't used to Deedee being the one to leave. In their unwritten agreement of friendship he was the wanderer and she was the homebody. Where could

she have disappeared to, and why didn't she call? He had
to stop himself from calling her daughter, whom he
didn't want to alarm. *If she doesn't come back by tomorrow
evening, I'll call Alma,* he determined. He swigged the last
of the beer and went outside to breath in the clear night
air. Was it something he'd said? Or perhaps something
he hadn't said? He'd finally found himself a suitable
partner, and now she was gone. He kicked the gravel on
the path and walked into the large thicket across the way.
If he called the police to report the disappearance of an
eighty-year-old woman who didn't even live in the area
they would alert all units, and everyone would think it
was another tragedy: an Alzheimer patient who couldn't
remember where she lived. The last thing he wanted to
see was a picture of Deedee Field alongside a picture of
an orange Mustang hanging on bulletin boards.

"I trust you, Deedee," he said, looking up to the sky.
"If you decided to get up and leave like that you must
have had a really good reason. But please… give me a
little sign, just a little sign to let me know you're all right.
Even a light rustling of the wind through the leaves of
that tree would be sufficient. Okay? I'm waiting. One,
two, three…" He paused for a long time, watching

expectantly, but not a single leaf shifted. When he grew tired he took a seat under the tree and continued watching its leaves. The night air smelled sweet and spicy with pollen and rain. His nostrils flared to take in the refreshing aroma. He always began to feel stifled after staying indoors for too long. The living room always had a smell, a kind of depressing mixture of dill and vinegar. He wondered if the smell was emanating from his eighty-seven-year-old body or from the walls and floors of the house, which had known better days. When Deedee was around, the fragrance of her apple pie coming from the kitchen concealed any bad odors.

When he grew tired of sitting, Wendell lay down on the moist ground and looked up at the few visible stars. He remembered how they'd lain together at the beach, watching the sky, on their way to Rosie's house. He had no idea that Deedee had been driving all day long, and that at the very moment when he was lying there, thinking about her, she'd arrived in Sullivan, Maine.

Rosie's house had remained precisely as they'd left it: dark and lifeless, but her sister's soul seemed to still dwell among inanimate objects. Deedee walked into the bedroom and opened the small window over the bed to let in some fresh air. She let down her hair over her wiry shoulders, then lay her head on Rosie's thick pillow. Now that she no longer had to remain alert to drive the car, she could finally sense how tired she was. She stared at the picture of goldfish that hung over the bed until she fell asleep.

Our big, magnificent existence is nothing but small moments.
Like loose pictures attached to a line with a clothespin.
A pretty collection which, at the end of time, at the end of the line,
Composes that vulnerable, unknowable thing
Which we call life…

The next morning Deedee woke up as the first rays of sun invaded the bedroom and immediately got out of bed. She went to her suitcase and found a thin white shirt and wide blue pants. Then she took a long, hot shower, reviving herself. *This, eventually, is what remains,* she thought as she dried herself and looked at her blurry reflection in the steamy mirror. *Little, transient things, against the backdrop of endless, eternal death. A nice hot shower, a*

good meal, a conversation with an old friend. She remembered
Wendell with a pang of longing. She hoped he'd
understand her sudden disappearance and wouldn't take
offence, and made a mental note to call him as soon as
she was finished washing up.

***

That morning Wendell woke up at the same time he
usually did and had breakfast alone. He was used to
living alone and liked to talk to himself a lot, especially
when his mind was racing. But today he said nothing,
staring out the window as he chewed his sandwich. After
he finished eating he went into his woodshop, grabbed a
small plank, and began to whittle it. He decided to build
a little wooden car for his grandson. He didn't know
when he would next see him, if at all, but the urge to
make a gift for him was too great to contain.

Though he'd made countless creations in his
woodshop, this was his first attempt at a toy car. He
quickly lost himself in planning and preparing, and for a
few moments was able to forget about Deedee's absence.
By the time he took a break it was late in the day. He sat
down on the bench outside and watched the last of the
sunlight swallowed by the lonesome melancholy of night.

Then he returned to his woodshop and turned on the lamp by his side. The toy car was almost finished. He buffed its edges for the last time and looked it over. It was so quiet outside that he could easily hear his own breath coming in and out and the toads croaking in the pond.

Ever since Deedee moved in the two of them liked to spend evenings sitting among the red rose bushes out front. Wendell usually solved crossword puzzles while Deedee read one of the novels she'd borrowed from the library. On occasion he interrupted her, asking for her help with the puzzle, and together they tried to solve it. These were moments of serenity, and the first time in a long time when he didn't feel the need to constantly keep busy, his soul yearning for a new place. Beating Deedee at scrabble and eating her apple pie were now the great things in his life.

He heard the phone ringing in the kitchen and rushed inside.

Hello Dear Sister,

We haven't seen each other in a long time, and I'm writing to tell you that, though we don't often speak, you are always in my heart.

We are now at the age when the complexity and difficulty of life are well-known to us, but it is simplicity which we have forgotten. Simple actions like calling you in the morning to tell you I've missed you and ask how you are doing have become cumbersome.

Why? I do not know.

I'm sorry I wasn't always a supportive sister to you. I can only tell you that you are the dearest person to me in this world.

I send my love to you, to Benjie, and to my beautiful niece.

Love you always,

Rosie.

It was a letter Rosie had written her long ago and, for some unknown reason, never sent. When Deedee packed up Rosie's things to give to charity she came across it, in a white envelope in a drawer. She held onto it for a long time, reading it over and over again, then slipped it into her suitcase. "I'm sorry I never had a chance to say goodbye, Rosie," she mumbled. She looked at the floor strewn with things and thought: *Or perhaps we'd already said goodbye long ago... whenever I thought about you, knowing you were here, eating dinner or reading one of your philosophy books or cookbooks before bed, I said goodbye to you and held you close to my heart. Goodbyes should be gradual, the heart can only handle a little at a time. Life is full of goodbyes. There, each day we say goodbye to the sun, which leaves a red trail of parting in its wake.*

Standing among the boxes of things and piles of books, Deedee asked herself how she'd gotten herself into this mess. She called Wendell and apologized for taking his car without asking for permission. "I went to pack up Rosie's house," she explained. "I needed to say goodbye quietly, by myself." Then she put her shoes on and went out for a walk. A warm spring breeze caressed her face and sent a tremor of longing through her, for what, she did not know.

When the body finishes its journey and returns to mother earth, the soul continues to the world of spirits, the great creation, and perhaps from there it goes on to another round. Who knows? There will be no other woman like Rosie in the history of this world. With all the billions of people being born and dying, there never was and never will be another like her.

In her hand, she was holding a small watercolor
Rosie had made of sailboats floating in a cerulean sea.
The contours were done in delicate brush strokes. Rosie
was not a pretty woman. She had a vulturine nose and
dark brown stick-like hair that fell on her face and made
her look frumpy. And yet, to Deedee she was beautiful
and unique, perhaps because Deedee could see what was
inside.

She sat down on a park bench, closed her eyes, and
took a deep breath. Then she crossed her arms and gave
herself a long hug. Snuggled into herself, she couldn't
remember the last time she'd showed herself such
kindness. It felt good.

***

It was getting late, but Wendell was still sitting on his
bench, waiting for her. The calls of a nocturnal bird
emerged from the deep silence, only to be swallowed in
the magical chill of night. He stepped inside for a
moment to get his sleeping bag, laid it out on the lawn,
and crawled into it. He slept like this for several hours
with a light breeze stroking his face, and woke up to the
familiar sounds of the engine groaning in the driveway.
He pulled himself out of the sleeping bag and stared at

the thick smoke that was emanating from the exhaust
pipe.

***

Long car rides are like meditations. Thoughts pass in and
out like the trees and the clouds. She drove and drove,
slowly and cautiously, never daring to go faster than
forty miles an hour, taking in the green meadows. Several
times she had to tame her urge to get off the freeway and
into one of the antique shops on the side of the road.
Whenever she felt tired she took a bite of the large
chocolate bar that rested on the passenger seat. When
she did this, she thought about how Wendell loved to
munch on cookies as he drove. It was a difficult drive,
dark roads in a moonless night. When she finally arrived,
exhausted, she advanced slowly over the dirt path,
holding her glasses to her nose, straining to see the
borders of the path. She didn't notice when she veered
off into the shallow ditch on the side of the road. Trying
to get out, she hit the gas pedal, but it was no good: both
front tires and one of the rear tires spun uselessly. The
engine began to groan and thick smoke bellowed.
Deedee stepped out of the car quickly as Wendell
hurried over, looking at the old car half-trapped and

half-hovering. She crossed her arms and said, "I'm sorry, Wendell… I, I don't know what to say."

"Don't apologize, the important thing is you made it home safe." He wrapped his arms around her.

She tried to smile, feeling her embarrassment grow as she searched for the right words.

Wendell looked at her tired face. She was holding her juicer in one hand and Rosie's art in the other. His heart went out to her. "Go on inside and make yourself a hot cup of tea," he said. "I'll figure out a way to get the car out of that ditch."

She dragged her feet inside, went into the bathroom, sat on the closed toilet lid and cried silently.

Wendell stood at the front of the car and shook it from side to side. Glancing at him through the bathroom window, Deedee saw the light from the lamp illuminating his white tuft of hair and unshaved face. He looked grave and dramatic, as befitted a man trying to release a stuck car. Then, for a moment, he almost seemed glad for the unexpected adventure that brought some excitement back into his life.

He realized that if one more tire touches the ground, he'd be able to push the car out of the ditch. He got inside, hit the gas, then stepped outside and shook the car again, surprised by how strong he still was at his age. Then, exhausted, he sat back down behind the wheel.

Deedee heard the engine growling. The car burrowed into the dirt, leaving a trail of dust behind it, then all at once began to move out of the ditch and onto the path.

His face beamed. He raised his sooty hands up into the air as he stepped out of the car and called out, "Deedee, Deedee, come look! Everything works out in the end!"

She stepped outside. "Good job," she said cheerfully as she limped over.

He smiled at her. His face was stained with tire grease. Then he looked back at the car and felt an immense relief at seeing it back in the driveway, safe and sound.

SUMMER

"Beer and pickles?" Deedee was standing at the doorway to the kitchen, wearing a thin floral dress. Her eyes were puffy with sleep. The remains of Wendell's dinner from the previous night were still on the table—a piece of dry rye bread with a thick layer of red jam, and a few partially peeled radishes. Above those, a few flies buzzed, searching for food and shelter from the heat.

She looked at the two empty beer bottles and at the large pickle jar floating with dill stems and cloves of garlic. Last night, Wendell thought it would be a good idea to eat pickles with his nightly beer. He ate and solved crossword puzzles in the kitchen until the middle of the night. She cleared the dishes from the table and wiped off the crumbs and sticky jam residue with a cloth.

On the living room table was a large jigsaw puzzle box—1,500 pieces. Many of these pieces were scattered around the box, sorted into small groups. On the back of the box was a colorful picture of a couple walking in a field of flowers, surrounded by butterflies. Wendell had bought the puzzle a week ago and was slowly putting it together. For many afternoons, his glasses resting on his nose, he connected tiny puzzle pieces, starting with the outer frame. It was the kind of thing he'd never allowed himself to do before, dedicating time to seemingly pointless endeavors. Thus early afternoon melted into dusk in divine peace. Sometimes it took him that entire time only to make one match, but he was always pleased with himself nonetheless.

"Pickles and a puzzle," Deedee said, smiling with her mouth full of grapefruit. "Is that what the elderly do?"

"Yes," he said, keeping his eyes on the puzzle. "Nagging old men who smell of pickles and dills. I can't get rid of that smell. Do you smell it?"

She took a few inhales and closed her eyes for better concentration. "I don't smell it," she said, shrugging and continuing to eat.

"Maybe it's just my body rotting, the smell of old age," he said unhappily.

She put her fork done. Her eyes were serious. "The smell of old age? I've never thought of that. Do I smell that way too?" she asked.

"Oh, no, of course not," he answered candidly. "You always smell fresh." But he could tell she didn't believe him.

"But I'm also, you know, not…"

"Not what?" he asked, regretting ever bringing it up.

"Not a young woman anymore."

He said nothing for a while. Then he fixed his burning eyes on her and said, "You smell better than any women I've ever met."

Morning sounds dripped in from outside, filling the kitchen.

"Deedee."

"Yes."

"What would you do if you knew you couldn't fail?"

"Me?"

Wendell nodded, looking into her eyes.

"Maybe I'd become a poet, like I always dreamed," she said after a while, turning her face away from him.

"You're already a poet. You write poems."

"Poems that no one has ever read."

"You can't let other people decide whether or not you're a poet. It's up to you."

"Years ago, when I was younger, I sent a few poems to a famous poet, to get his opinion. He wrote me back, a very enthusiastic letter, asking me to send him some more, and even offering to help me get a few poems published in a literary magazine. I was so scared by the idea of publishing that I had an anxiety attack and had to lie in bed for days. I finally thanked him and promised to send more poems, but I never did. How odd. The possibility of succeeding and connecting with others frightened me more than the chance of failure. What about you? What would you do if you knew you couldn't fail?"

He cleared his throat and shifted uncomfortably in his seat. "I... it's obvious. I would have never abandoned my son."

Dandelions in the Wind

By Deedee Field

After the long winter,
Yellow dandelions appeared all at once.
Their short season disrupts their beauty.
When their petals turn white.

We will also scatter

On the great wind.

Did we remember to make a wish?

***

On July 27th, an exceptionally hot day, in the early afternoon, with the ground boiling beneath her feet, Deedee walked quickly onto the lawn and to the old shed. The saw Wendell used was on the floor among other scattered work tools, and the smell of hot sawdust was in the air. Not having found him, she walked back outside, wondering where he could have gone in this heat. She walked to the pond, called his name a few times, but received no answer. Other than a few sleepy toads hiding in the water and some buzzing insects, the place was still.

She sat down on the bench. The air was humid, gluing her clothes to her body. She decided not to think about the poems she'd sent out to a publisher that morning. She'd gathered her courage and gone to the post office with three poems sealed in a brown manila envelope. For the first time in a long time, or perhaps ever, she felt content. She'd finally dared take this step. Whatever happened next, she knew, didn't matter. She was beginning to sink into a pleasant drowsiness. Her straw hat covered her face, and her awareness was drifting in and out when suddenly she heard Wendell's voice. She opened her eyes and found him standing before her, his face flushed and sweaty. He looked worse than she'd ever seen him.

"This is one of the shittiest days of my life, let me tell you."

She sat up at once, fixed her hat and looked him over. He was wearing a red plaid shirt and his black baseball cap. His face, which normally beamed, was crestfallen, and the flames in his eyes had gone out. "What happened?" she asked, alarmed. "You look terrible."

"This morning at six I went to the woodshop as usual. I was buffing the knob I'd made for the kitchen drawer. Then as I crossed the room I just fell to the floor." He sat down on the bench next to her and offered his right arm. It had a reddish purple hemorrhage on it. "My knees just buckled and I couldn't do anything about it." Then he fell silent and stared straight ahead. His face was pained.

Deedee put her hand over his and said nothing.

"I always told myself I wasn't planning on getting old, but I guess no one asked me."

They never mentioned his fall again for the rest of the summer. Wendell also didn't share the other times he'd taken a plunge during his morning walks. He accepted the situation, training himself like one might a puppy, to focus his attention on the good things in his life. He became a champion jigsaw puzzle solver and addict, behaving as if God himself was hiding among the pieces on the table. They all looked the same to him until that magical moment in which they came together to form a glorious work of art.

"That's a beautiful picture," Deedee said, looking at the finished, colorful puzzle. It was a picture of a woman in a yellow wide-brimmed hat and a handsome middle aged man sitting on a picnic blanket, surrounded by a blossoming grassy knoll. They were holding two glasses of wine and looking at each other with shy smiles. It was one of those impressionistic images she had a feeling she'd seen before. Maybe Renoir, or another painter from the same time period, she couldn't say for sure. "They tried to capture the fleeting moment, these impressionist painters," she told Wendell. "A fraction of a second when two people sat together, talking. That was their focus."

"In that case they've succeeded, each moment of putting together this puzzle felt like eternity," he quipped.

"I've always admired your tenacity," Deedee said, leaning against the back of the brown chair, sipping her tea. She was wearing light colored clothes, and her face was pale.

Wendell looked at her. Her eyes seemed different that morning. "Are you feeling all right?" he asked.

"I think so. Just tired. I woke up in the middle of the night from an unpleasant dream and couldn't go back to sleep."

Her skin was almost translucent, her cheeks covered in gray patches. "Should we go see a doctor?" he asked hesitantly, trying to conceal his concern.

"Oh, that won't be necessary. I'm just tired. It'll pass." She knew he didn't believe her. "I think I just had too many sad thoughts before bed. It takes a toll, you know."

"What did you think about?"

"About Alma, and the fact that we haven't seen each

other in almost a year. The distance between us is more than geographical. There's also a great emotional distance." She sighed, closed her eyes, and lingered that way. Then she opened her eyes and looked at him.

"I think that's just the way life is," he said.

"Not for everybody," she said quietly. "Not everyone lives so far away from their parents."

"Yes, that's true," he said. "Not for everybody, but for most people."

"Are you sure?"

"I don't know… but I think so." They sat together on the sofa and he put his arm around her shoulder.

"You know," she said, "when I was at Rosie's house I tried to picture her lying in bed during the last night of her life. I wanted to know what she felt. Did she wake up a moment before death, knowing that something was about to happen?"

He stood up and offered his hand. "Come on," he said. "Let's go into town to watch an animated movie, and then we can go have some apple pie."

She took his hand and rose to her feet heavily. "You're a very special man, Wendell Parker," she said, squeezing his hand.

That evening, when they returned home, Deedee picked up the water hose and watered the flowerbed. She continued to water it even after the ground was already drenched and overflowing.

"Hey, Deedee, that's a lot of water," Wendell called out. "I think you can stop watering now…"

She looked at him as if she'd just woken up from a dream. "Oh, you're right. I didn't notice. I was thinking," she said. Then she moved the hose and accidentally sprayed him. The sensation of the cold water made Wendell jump. "Oh my God, I'm so sorry!" Deedee cried. "I'll go get you a towel."

When she turned toward the house, Wendell picked up the hose, the water still flowing, and called, "Hey, Deedee!"

When she turned around the water hit her straight on. She closed her eyes, wiped her face with her hand, and felt a creeping insult taking over her, unsure whether to smile or frown. Then she went to Wendell, pulled the hose from his hand, and sprayed his legs, then his head.

He turned his back and started hopping, flinching at the cold water. "Stop it, Deedee, stop it! It's too cold, Deedee!" He tried to run away and she chased him, aiming the hose as if it were a gun. When she finally stopped, Wendell ran, wet and defeated, to shut off the water. The ground all around them was swampy, and Wendell's hair stuck up, making him look like a miserable street cat who'd fallen into a puddle.

They looked at each other, panting, their clothes dripping, and their eyes smiling. Then they both broke out into a rolling laughter, two children, their wrinkles glowing beneath the wetness. She couldn't remember the last time she'd laughed like that.

"Even my underwear is wet," said Wendell. "I'll have to pry it out of my droopy butt."

That brought on another uncontrollable surge of laughter.

As they walked inside, Wendell removed his drenched clothes and his muddy socks at the door. Deedee caught a glimpse of his naked body as he hurried into the bathroom. Then she went into her bedroom to change her clothes, and on her way to the laundry room picked up his clothes off the floor, too.

***

That night, Deedee dreamt she was sitting in a small sailboat, surrounded by an endless black ocean. She was sailing to meet Alma, who lived on the other shore. A light breeze blew into her overloaded heart, refreshing its hidden treasures.

When the wind grew stronger, she knew she had to spread the sails and began fighting with the ropes, not knowing which way to pull. The boat was tipping, dragged in the wrong direction. She pulled and moved the ropes until the boat finally tilted upright. Then she saw Benjie looking at her with his big, brown eyes, and calling to her, his voice distant and muffled: "Deedee, I'm so proud of you."

The little sailboat continued to float over the deep water, tilting this way and that. She watched Benjie's image growing distant and wanted to tell him something, but couldn't make a sound. All she wanted was to see her daughter and put her arms around her, but the wind was starting up again and the boat began to veer off course once more.

She had so much to say to Wendell. Her heart yearned for him and Alma. If she only could, she would get off this boat and run to them to tell them how much she loved them.

"When you reach the shore, Sis, we can play together again, like we used to. Remember when we were little and hid beneath that heavy blanket, pretending no one could ever find us?"

"Rosie," Deedee smiled. "My dear Rosie... it's been so long since we've played. Things used to be simple. Why did they have to change? Did we let go of love as we grew older, allowing it to become a momentary luxury?"

The sailboat continued to pull away from the shore, but Deedee was no longer fighting it. Instead, she lay on her back and allowed the wind to take her wherever it chose. She listened to the waves whispering the secrets of life and death, which dwelled within them, side by side. Then she felt Rosie growing closer, embracing her.

"We're like flowers," Rosie whispered. "We bloom for a moment, and then we wilt, but we leave traces of beauty and grace behind us."

A great sense of serenity was filling Deedee's heart. She felt as if she were floating along a clear lake, letting its pure water wash softly over her. She hugged Rosie back. A bright light surrounded them, painting a blinding white trail across the dark ocean water. Like a bird hovering above the surface, she said goodbye to the people she used to love so much it hurt. Now she too was returning to that place where there is no beginning and no end, no pleasure and no pain, no fear and no bravery, no doubt and no faith, and, most importantly: no more loneliness. Forever.

***

Just as the trees and flowers reached full bloom, as the generous sun warmed the world lavishly like a mother hugging her children, among the humming of insects and buzzing of bees in the fields, Deedee left this world.

The next morning, Wendell woke up at 4:30. He looked around at the darkness that still enveloped the land, and listened to his beloved silence. Then he spread a mat and did a headstand. This had been his daily habit for forty years: three minutes in which his blood flowed from his feet to his head.

When he finished, he took a leisurely morning walk, carefully making his way through the chill of night that lingered. "Autumn will come soon and it'll be too cold to stroll like this," he thought out loud, buttoning up his cardigan. When he turned around a loud caw of a crow sliced through the air from the nearby fields. *How strange,* he thought. *I've never heard crows here before.* He looked up to the sky and searched for the crow. The sky was clear, not a cloud in sight. Sometimes it seemed that summer would fight autumn to the death.

When he returned home he read the morning paper, scanning the sports section, and slicing a piece of apple pie, to enjoy with another cup of tea. A different kind of quiet filled the house. It was as if time stood still. He glanced at his watch. It was 8:40. He wondered if Deedee was awake. She usually woke up before he did.

When he finished his breakfast he went into his woodshop. The blue bench he'd been working on for the past few months was finished, and the smell of fresh paint filled the air. He looked at his creation with satisfaction. "You did a fine job here," Mr. Parker, he said to himself as he carried the bench outside and placed it at the center of the garden, among the white and yellow flowers. He sat down slowly, leaned back, folded his arms in his lap, and glanced at the kitchen windows, his eyes searching for her. Judging by the sun on his face, he knew it was getting late, and for a moment his heart ached. He wanted to get up, but something inside of him told him to stay there. His body was petrified, his rear end glued to the bench.

He didn't know how much time had passed before he finally took a deep breath and told himself through a dry throat: "Come on, old sport, there's no choice. Go in there and wake her up. How long can one person sleep?"

He got up on his feet and walked quickly into the house. He knocked softly on Deedee's door and opened it slowly. She was lying on her back, her eyes closed, her long hair framing her face. One look was enough for him to know she was no longer there. Her thin body lay lifeless, like the cocoon of a caterpillar after the butterfly had flown out. The Deedee he'd known was elsewhere.

He lay on the floor at her feet and tucked his knees into his chest, curling like a fetus. He cried deep, silent tears, his entire body convulsing. He lay there for a long time, weeping like a little boy who was left alone in the world. Then he pulled himself together, got up, walked over, and gave her a long kiss on the cheek.

***

To: Mrs. Deedee Field

<u>*Re: Poems for Publication*</u>

Dear Mrs. Field,

We'd like to thank you for sharing your poetry with us. We found it to be well-wrought and lucid, often saturated with sadness, and expertly depicting the experience of parting, which we all participate in at certain moments in our lives. We are thrilled to send you the September issue of our journal, which includes one of your poems.

Sincerely,

The Editors

Goodbye

The people I once loved are all gone.

Some of them have returned their souls and bodies to the great lap of creation.

Others have continued in their convoluted journey down the paths of life.

And my little heart, still beating, has grown old,

Filling with yearning for them all,

Maintaining their long lost identity,

Like a child guarding a fragile treasure.

Of all the moments of life I've lived beside them, goodbye is the hardest of all.

Deedee Field, 1933-2013